Tsar Alexei II

At The Millennium

By J.M. Carns

To

Alexei Nikolaevich Romanov

Who Touched Our Hearts

And My Mom for Reading My Stories

Table of Contents

Author's Prologue

This story is a sequel to *Tsar Alexei II Could History Be Different? Could Russia Be Saved?* This story is based off the alternative history of the original story where Alexei is abducted by the Provisional Government and made the figurehead Tsar. Elements of this story may not be understood without reading the original story. There are also spoilers to the original story in this story. James will be the narrator of this story, a wealthy yet lonely young man in Santa Cruz California. He has finished his last year of high school and is approaching his 19th birthday in the year 2000. Tsar Alexei II is his idol whom he totally adores, and he knows everything about. While our first story was intended as a more serious piece of alternative history, this story will be more fanciful and allegorical. Credit for any historical research was given in the original story. Now let's read as Tsar Alexei II comes alive through James's eyes.

Chapter 1

I was sitting at the Santa Cruz Public Library as usual, a boring mid-century California style building, researching my favorite topic, Tsar Alexei II, the last Tsar of Russia. My last year of high school had just ended, and the long boring summer was about to begin. Alexei had been my history fair project. I knew everything there was to know about him, and totally adored him. If only Alexei had lived, I know he could have saved Russia. He was a true leader. He had all the right answers. The people loved him and still do love him. If only the evil commie bastards had not murdered him. Though I guess the right wing could have murdered him as well, for his vision of equality, land reform, and taxing the rich to help the poor.

I often fantasized myself as Sergei, locked with Alexei in the Winter Palace, then under unofficial house arrest with him at the Alexander Palace. That must have been so much fun, getting Alexei largely to himself for so many years. They were so close, they even slept in the same bed. Sergei only passed away last year and was dedicated to the memory of his friend to his dying breath. Sergei never married or had kids. He could never move past his devotion to Alexei. How wonderful those years they spent together must have been. If only Alexei, with all his warmth, kindness and empathy had been my friend, instead of those jerks at my high school, maybe I wouldn't have felt so alone. If I had one and only one wish, it would be to save Alexei, for Alexei to have lived. The horrors of communism would have never happened, and the fascist reaction would have been prevented, no World War II, no Cold War, what a better place this world would be.

If only Alexei had lived, if only Alexei had lived. If only Alexei had lived. I sat on the stool, at the big old computer monitor and keyboard, typing over and over again, "How could I save Tsar Alexei II." Some interesting stuff about Alexei came up, much of it I had seen before, and some random weird shit came up. Even some sick psychopath came up about how great it was Alexei was murdered, with some pretty disgusting graphic fantasies about his death. I wanted to reach through the computer screen and beat this anonymous asshole senseless.

Then I simmered down and settled back into my seat, with my personal book I had brought with me in my backpack, "Alexei in Pictures." Going over the photos of Alexei, with the old grainy image and a touched up colorized version, side by side, always cheered me up. I especially enjoyed the more intimate photos of Alexei with his family and friends.

As I was reading this very non-descript little man with white hair and a worn brown suit walked up to me. He looked older than dirt. He had a certain smirk on his face, but he intrigued me. He just seemed a bit out of place for somebody in the library in Santa Cruz California.

Old Man, "Hello James, I see you are a fan of Alexei's."

Now I was totally creeped out, how in the hell did this guy who I have never seen know my name. "Huh, who are you?"

Old Man, "That is unimportant, what is important is what I can do for you."

With a sense of sarcasm in my voice, "Okay, I will bite, what can you do for me?"

Old Man, "You want to save Alexei, I can grant you that wish, well I cannot do it for you, but I can provide you the tool to achieve that."

I was feeling now even a little more creeped out, how did he know I wanted to save Alexei, I mean I had the photo book of Alexei in front of me, but was he watching me, had he somehow hacked my searches, who was this strange little man, I then retorted, "Is this some sort of practical joke, who put you up to this?"

Old Man, "I never joke," he then pulled out an intricately carved piece of wood with a dragon's head on top, it looked so old and warped, almost like driftwood, he then continued, "This has been around a very long time, it allows the owner to travel through time, anywhere any place, you only hold it firmly, think about where you want to go and it will take you. But be careful you do not lose it on your journeys, otherwise you will not be coming home. You can go back in time, you can save Alexei, he needs you. This is your destiny."

I would just have loved to save Alexei, but I broke out laughing hysterically, "Sir the mental health clinic is a few blocks down."

The man smirked again, "I will be leaving shortly, but I think you know in your heart what you want to do. You really think I randomly picked you? He then handed me the piece of wood. The choice is yours, will your beloved Alexei live, or will you let him die again, and again, and again?"

I took a look at it confounded, and when I looked up, he was gone.

Okay I thought to myself, now if I wanted to travel in time why would I want to watch Alexei get shot, I would prefer to go to the Alexander Palace before Alexei stood up to Kerensky and just hang out with him and Sergei. Maybe Kerensky's handpicked friends for Alexei could drop by. Oleg always seemed like an interesting enough character. But then how would I explain myself, they would probably have me arrested and locked up in the nuthouse. I then realized I was thinking crazy, as if this was real.

Well, I figured, okay let's prove this fake once and for all. I was ready for some of the boys from my high school to come out from behind the bright yellow bookshelves laughing hysterically, the assholes probably put their grandfather up to this or something. Everyone knew how into Alexei I was, in fact it was practically a school joke.

I grasped the wooden thing, and thought to myself, "Okay God of driftwood, take me back to Ekaterinburg July 17th, 1923, as Alexei is giving his famous speech."

And then I was there, the little train station, the adoring crowds, the early 20th century buildings, with the forest in the backdrop, Alexei was on the platform in that olive green army uniform with the red bars on his shoulders, giving his speech in Russian. I just realized of course this wouldn't be in English, but I knew Alexei's speech from heart, he was so handsome, and alive, and full of energy, how could some sick, depraved sniper be preparing to shoot this great man.

And then the fear slipped into me, what the fuck, am I dreaming, am I insane, is this real? Maybe it is time for a mental health checkup. And then I thought to myself home again, and I was back at the library. Did anybody see me appear and disappear, here, in Ekaterinburg, what about my out-of-place wardrobe, my blue jeans, pale green polo shirt and white sneakers? But this could not be real. I decided it was time to walk home before I drew any more attention to myself, maybe I just needed to take a nap.

I walked home through the quaint tree lined streets of Santa Cruz, houses of early 20th century stock, a mixture of homes with Victorian and Bungalow influences. It was a beautiful late May day, the sun was out and warm. However, I could hardly pay attention to any of it, as I thought in bewilderment what was happening. I walked up to my parents' quaint million-dollar bungalow, this is Santa Cruz after all, and went up the front steps in the door.

I had the house all to myself as usual. My dad a banker spent much of his time in San Jose, and my mom doing whatever her project of the month was. I was an only child. I tossed the frozen fried clams in the oven with the French fries, and made my favorite dip, a mixture of condiments, spices, and dried herbs. As it baked, I continued to think. When done I tossed it all on the plate and headed up to my room. It was the typical room of a nerdy 1990s rich kid with my bed, my dresser, and my big old computer with the tower at the desk. Well not totally typical. I had all the books on Alexei, and several posters of him on the wall, but why would I want some rock band when I could have an inspirational figure like Alexei.

As I ate my lunch, I sat on my bed thinking. And I thought to myself, it seemed so real, did it really matter if it was real, what was reality anyway. Maybe I should just play this out, maybe I can save Alexei. What do I have to lose. But I needed a plan. There has been speculation, but nobody knew the exact position of the assassin or assassins. And if I confronted them, if they can kill the Tsar of Russia, what would happen to me. What happens if you die traveling back in time, I didn't really want to find out. I had to come up with a plan.

Then it dawned on me. I would take my father's gun and shoot at the platform. The guards would likely grab Alexei and pull him to safety, before the real assassins could get him. Might be a bit risky, but if I wished myself back at that minute, what could happen to me. Alexei would be alive, and the world would be saved. But I needed a change of clothes, my jeans, polo shirt, and sneakers stood out too much. I dressed in my khaki pants, white oxford, and dress shoes, yeah, a little out of place, but not as much. I got my father's gun out of his closet, carefully remembered exactly where everything was to put it back, went back to my room and figured okay, time to change history. Time to save my dear sweet Alexei.

Back to Ekaterinburg, and there I was, I slipped around the side of the train depot, so I could not completely be seen. And there once again was Alexei. I really needed to learn Russian, I figured, but as I said, I knew the speech by heart. I wanted to hang out in the crowd, shake his hand, hug him, meet him, but I was here on a mission, and if not successful, he was going to be dead shortly. He just oozed warmth, his presence, in person it felt as if you were being touched by God. He was not perfectly polished, but he had sincerity. I felt in that moment what you cannot get out of a book. I didn't want this moment to end, but I knew it must. I gripped the stick, pulled out the gun, and fired at the platform, having exactly the effect I thought it would, they grabbed Alexei scrambling towards the train, this was way too easy, and then I thought home, and there I was.

And there I was back in my bedroom, but this was not my bedroom, I felt suddenly terrified, grabbed a backpack that didn't look like mine, shoved the gun in it, and walked out, this was my house, but it was not my house, I walked out on to the street, it was very much my street, but some things were vaguely different. I ran to the library, all the way noticing things were very much the same, but they were not the same.

As I entered the library I got on the computer. Things somewhat played out as they had in history, which I could not understand. Saving Alexei was going to save the world. Then as I dug deeper, I saw that after the second assassination attempt on Alexei, Kerensky had them locked in their compartments and taken back to Petrograd (St

Petersburg), where Alexei was forcefully held at the Alexander Palace and not allowed to leave. The government lasted another two years, and Kerensky took Alexei into exile when he fled.

Ultimately after spending a few months with his family at some country estate in Britain, Alexei got bored and became the resistance to Stalin in exile. As he watched a play in London, a Soviet agent shot him in the back of the head, killing him instantly. Alexei still died and history was not that different. I realized Alexei was never going to stop standing up for what he felt was right, and they were going to kill him for it. I also noticed, Alexei, though still fondly remembered by many, his legacy was not as pronounced. The Communists never co-opted his memory.

Then I realized the big difference, Russia was not as prepared for World War II, as the Communists had consolidated later. Germany drove deeper into Russia, Britain had been hit harder, the war ended in 1947, not 1945, and Berlin had also been nuked. And then I realized in 1946 my grandfather's regiment had been wiped out. My mom did not exist, I did not exist. I was here, but I did not exist. Wow, that threw me for a loop.

Okay time to fix this now. I grabbed the satanic stick, and immediately put myself back to Ekaterinburg, right before I pulled the trigger, I decided to not pull the trigger, I didn't even take time to admire Alexei, I grabbed the stick once again, and I figured hey I can go wherever I want, no reason to walk home, and put myself right back in my bedroom. It was the same as it was before I tried to change history. I collapsed on the bed with a sigh of relief, my heart still about ready to jump out of my body.

I quickly put the gun back up in my father's closet then went back to my room. I was kind of sad. I had failed to save Alexei and had almost wiped myself out of existence. Alexei still died, World War II went on longer, millions more died, but history in the end was not that different, well for the world, it was very different for me. I drifted off a bit and woke up mid-afternoon, feeling a little better. And then it dawned on me, if I could take the gun through history maybe I could take other things, maybe I could take people. Maybe I could take Alexei. If he couldn't live in his timeline, maybe he could live in mine. Alexei could be the best friend I always wanted, he would be mine. My warm, kind, empathetic, fun-loving Alexei, we would have one hell of a time.

But I had to be careful about it, if I didn't want to alter history too much, I didn't want to try that again. And I had to think about how I did it, it couldn't seem like some strange guy from the future abducted Alexei, that might alter history in itself. And how would I approach Alexei, I didn't want to scare him, he would probably think I was a nutter.

And I would have to get to him before he called for the guard. Maybe if I got into his sleeping compartment the night before the assassination, I mean he would be exiting his timeline about the same time he really did. How much harm could that cause?

I was tired, but I couldn't wait to see Alexei, and so I tried it again, but this time I catapulted into Alexei's sleeping compartment slightly after midnight on July 17th. And there he was close up, alone in the flesh, not grainy old photos, or photoshopped images, but the real Alexei, skin blemishes and all. He was still in uniform and hadn't quite gotten into his night gown yet. He looked at me with a shocked look on his face like he was about to scream, and I put my finger to my lips.

Me, "Please do not be afraid Alexei, I'm here to save you. You're going to be assassinated this morning, but I can bring you with me."

Alexei, looking perplexed at me with his blue eyes. "Are you my guardian angel, or is this a dream?"

Me, "Neither, but I'm not sure if you will believe me, let me show you, you know I didn't come through that door, and if I wanted to hurt you, I would have, trust me."

Alexei, "Something about your dress is a little off, and your English though a bit different is good."

Alexei had always been said to speak perfect English,

but it sounded a little different, he sounded a bit like a Brit and a bit of something else, but he didn't have a stereotypical thick Russian accent.

Alexei then got up and opened the door, I froze in terror, as he said something in Russian. He then locked the door and spoke to me, "I just told the guard I am very tired and do not wish to be disturbed tonight," then Alexei sat down on the bed still very clearly pondering me. His lack of fear surprised me, but he was looking at me like a riddle he couldn't solve. "If you are not an angel, or a dream, exactly how do you know I am going to be assassinated tomorrow?" he said in a low voice. "The door is locked, they have been told not to disturb me, you are not in any danger."

I sat down in the chair next to his bed, "I'm from Santa Cruz California, the year 2000, you are my hero, I traveled here in time to save you."

Alexei smirked, "That is an amusing thought, thank you for lightening up my night, I am not sure how you slipped on my train, but I will make sure they do not hurt you. But I really ought to get some rest. I will get the guards to find you a place to sleep, and you can have breakfast with us in the morning. We will chat more then. I cannot wait to show you to Sergei, Kolya and Oleg, it will be fun."

I was touched by his kind gracious presence, he was everything I thought he would be, he clearly thought I was an intruder but was going to get me a place to sleep and invite me to breakfast with his friends in the morning. As much as I wanted to stay, I knew we had better go. He looked like he was about to get up and open the door. I then said, "Well okay, you don't believe me, but if I am lying you have nothing to lose if I try."

Alexei now with a full-toothed smile, "On one condition, then you will go to bed."

Me, "Yes, you have my word, if we fail, I will go to bed."

Alexei, "What do I need to do?"

Me, "I need to hold on to you, and with this short wand looking like thing, I will take us to my home."

Alexei got up, gave me a hug, and chuckled a bit. "Does this work?"

I felt better than I had felt my entire life up to that point. Alexei, hugging me, I truly felt his warmth. I loved him so much. I then said, "I think that will do," and wished us back to my bedroom in the year 2000 in Santa Cruz California.

Chapter 2

And there we were standing in my bedroom. Alexei was now looking a little scared, as he was looking around, and sat down on my bed. Everything was the same, so far nothing was different.

Me, "Give me a minute," as I sat down and dialed up the AOL connection, "Just making sure nothing really bad happened."

Alexei, "Huh," with a look between perplexment and fear on his face.

Me, "Well this doesn't always go well, but so far all looks good."

Alexei, "Now you tell me. You have done this before?"

As I was pulling up the internet, Alexei was zeroing in on my various posters of him.

Alexei, "You are quite an admirer of mine, those look like a cross of a photograph and a painting, but they look so real, but still are not quite me."

Me, "Those are old photos that have been colored by a modern process, because the old photos don't have color in them, there is a little bit of guesswork, we have accounts, and because you are so well known, close to contemporary times, we have a good idea on the colors, but it is not exact. And yes, I do love and admire you, you are my favorite person in the whole world, you were such a good guy."

Alexei, "Thank you for your kind words, I try to have the courage to do what is right."

I was a little perplexed by the words, "try to have the courage," he oozed courage, it seemed to come so naturally to him. Otherwise, how else could he have so continually exposed himself to possible harm. I looked up everything and nothing had changed, it looked as though he had been shot on the platform in Ekaterinburg, just like he really was, nothing was different, but oddly he was still here with me. I did not quite understand it. But I could not hope for a better outcome, nothing changed, but here was Alexei sitting on my bed very much alive. I had saved Alexei, and he was all mine.

Me, "Don't worry, everything is okay, nothing has changed."

Alexei, "What is that?" pointing at the computer.

I was thinking hard, now how was I going to explain a computer, to Alexei, "This is a computer, imagine an encyclopedia set, books, newspaper articles, I pull a lot of that up on this, without having to have to buy it, order it, fill my room up with it."

Alexei, "It is like a typewriter and a film, but you choose what you want to see."

Me, "Yes you could put it that way."

Alexei, "It is magic, this is all magic, like when Father Grigori saved my life, it is like I am in heaven, but this is not quite how I pictured heaven."

I pointed at the computer, "That is science," then I held up the time travel wand, "This I really don't know what this is."

Alexei, "It is God, it is all God, trust in God, his will, will be done."

This was Santa Cruz California in the year 2000, and I had never encountered someone close up with such a literal belief in God, my family was liberals, we did not hate God, we didn't necessarily disbelieve in him, but we did not really believe either, at least in such a literal sense. I knew Alexei was religious, but I never quite grasped the depth of his faith. I always saw Alexei as a reformer, as a liberal, he was the head of the Provisional Government, and they attempted so many liberal reforms before the Commies relegated them to the ash heap of history. It was such an optimistic moment, and Alexei sat on top of it all. In his speeches he clearly believed in equality of all, and a new Russia. Even though most accept Lenin killed him, there are even some theories the Monarchists did it because they felt he was too much a threat to the old order. But something about this Alexei had a conservative feel to him, almost backward and deeply superstitious. But then when I got up this morning, I would have thought time travel was absurd. What the hell did I know. I loved Alexei, and I wasn't going to challenge his faith.

Me, "Maybe."

He laid back on the bed in deep contemplation. And I laid back with him pondering his handsome face, his grayish blue eyes, his auburn brown hair, he was slightly tanned, but his gait, his posture, he was a bit awkward, if you paid enough attention, he almost seemed slightly crippled. He was six feet, two inches tall, slightly taller than me, but he was a bit spindly. I knew he was not some athlete, but his slight frailness still surprised me. I almost felt I could beat him up if I tried, me the wimp. But he was just as handsome as I pictured him, and he had this magnetic draw, even beyond his revered status in history.

Alexei, "You said nothing has changed, exactly what do you mean by that?"

Me, "Well it's a long story."

Alexei, "It does not feel like I am going anywhere any time soon."

I then explained it all to him, the real history, Stalin, the purges, the next great war, the fall of communism, and a very broad scope of what had happened to the world. I then explained the old man, the magic time travel wand, my initial fear, the consequences of saving him in his time, my last attempt where I brought him with me, and that absolutely nothing else had changed. Alexei was contemplative, I just loved that look on his face as he was thinking, it had such depth.

A broad smile crossed Alexei's face, I think the first time I had seen him smile since I brought him here, in that moment it felt as if I was the one in heaven.

Alexei, "Let's bring Sergei, and Kolya, and maybe I can convince Oleg to come, and Mr. Gilliard, and Dr. Derevenko, and my family of course."

I then felt a bit of frustration, "My parents will be so happy I have a friend, they will let you stay here, they will probably kiss your feet, but I can't keep them all, and I grabbed you right before your fate, that must be why nothing changed, if we go get them, it could have unintended consequences."

Alexei, "We will figure it out, and we could go get them right before their fates, like me."

Me, "They were largely pretty old, it will not be the same, it will be like an old-folks home. You died so young."

Alexei, "What is an old-folks home?"

Me, "It's where we put old people who can no longer care for themselves."

Alexei, "Their family does not take care of them?"

Me, "People are busy."

Alexei, "That is sad. How can this be heaven if I cannot have my family and friends?"

The smile had vanished from Alexei's face, I thought he was going to cry, I felt so sad, I loved him, I so wanted to comfort him, I did not want him to be sad. It never occurred to me he might be lonely. I had never had anyone, I would have loved to have been beamed into the Alexander Palace to spend my days with him. Yeah, I knew my parents loved me, but they spent so little time with me, I wouldn't really miss them. With Alexei, I felt less alone than I ever had, I so wanted to be his friend. But I didn't respond to him, I really didn't know what to say.

Alexei, not pushing the previous question, "You do not have any friends?"

Me, "No, the other students are jerks, I really hate them."

Alexei, "I guess I can see why they are not your friends if you hate them. I could be a rude little kid, but I do not think I have ever hated anyone in my life. I was isolated, but my parents and then Mr. Kerensky made sure I always had a few friends."

Me, "You were the Tsarevich, and then the Tsar, everybody loved, adored you, practically worshipped you, it was different."

Alexei, "Maybe."

We then just laid there in silence.

Then all of a sudden like magic, Alexei perked up and turned towards me smiling from ear to ear. His teeth were not perfect, and there was a gap between his two front teeth, but pretty good without orthodontia or modern dental care.

Alexei, "We will continue to discuss how to get the others here, but enough seriousness, I think we have had enough seriousness to last us a lifetime. If this is heaven it is time to have some fun, otherwise you might as well take me back to Ekaterinburg to get shot in the back. You say this is the year 2000, and we are on the California coast, from what I can see so far, you fellows must have invented some fun things to entertain yourselves."

Then a big smile crossed my face as I looked at him, I was so happy, I didn't know how we were possibly going to collect all the people Alexei had in mind, but maybe in time I could make him happy. He clearly wanted to be happy, to have a good time. And beyond Alexei's initial letdown, I was having the time of my life. I then thought about all the things I could do with Alexei, all the things he had never seen. The possibilities seemed endless. This was going to be the summer of my life. In this moment I didn't want to go to college anymore, I just wanted to hang out with Alexei forever, and ever.

Me, "There's so much, you will love it all, let me

think. I will take you to the Boardwalk tomorrow, let's just go downstairs and watch T.V. for now, you will love it. I'm pretty tired after today."

Alexei, "You got me right before bed and you are tired?"

Me, "Yeah, I thought you were tired too, you were the one telling me to go to bed."

Alexei, "Yeah, I am not really tired anymore, but we will watch this whatever you call it, if you want."

Me, "It is like a silent film, but with color and sound."

Alexei, "Wow, yeah, that sounds like fun."

We walked down the stairs and my mom in her dress suit walked in the door. I hadn't realized how late it had gotten. Alexei was still in uniform. Alexei walked right up to her and shook her hand.

"Hello madam, I am Alexei, I am just getting to know your son. Thank you so much for so graciously having me in your home."

My mom chuckled, "You're Alexei Romanov?"

Alexei, "Well, I am playing Alexei Romanov in a play, he is a distant cousin of mine. My name is Alexei Derevenko. I am visiting from Russia."

Mom, "Oh, I can see what drew James to you, but I am glad James has found a friend."

Alexei, "James is a great fellow, he is teaching me

everything about your lovely community."

Mom, "You're so polite, they must raise you Russian boys well, but your accent sounds more like a Brit though muddled with a little something else. But your English is perfect."

Alexei, "My grandma was English, my mom raised us speaking English, my dad spoke to us in Russian. My tutor taught me French as well."

Mom, "Sounds like you are a son of privilege and culture, give my regards to your parents, for a job well done, maybe some of you will rub off on James. And boy you are the spitting image of Alexei Romanov, I can see why you play him. You're sure he is only a distant cousin?"

Alexei, "Thank you madam, and yes, I am pretty sure."

Mom, "I'm warming up lasagna, I would be honored for you and James to join me for dinner."

I was a little confounded, my mom had not uttered a word to me, as Alexei charmed her. My mom and I didn't eat dinner together very often. But here comes Alexei barreling through time and my own mother already seems to prefer him to me. I felt a tinge of jealousy towards him at that moment. But I tried to look on the bright side, now I was sure she would let him stay as long as he wanted. Then we sat down for dinner. Alexei clearly loved the lasagna, something he had never had before. Alexei asked my mom about her activities and regaled her with his tales of his life in Russia.

Mom, "There's something about the Russia you describe that doesn't seem quite modern."

Alexei, "We are a backward country, but we try, I have had a very privileged life, but I feel very bad for those who are suffering. You get out of Petrograd, the poverty is shocking, and heartbreaking."

Mom, "You mean St. Petersburg?"

Alexei, "Yes, I am sorry, my family always liked the name Petrograd, it connects us with our Russian roots."

Mom, "It wouldn't surprise me if you were the President of Russia someday."

Alexei just smiled.

Me, "Mom can Alexei and I watch the big T.V.?"

Mom, "Of course, I'm going to bed, if Alexei is staying the night, make sure you boys play safe." She then went to shake Alexei's hand, and Alexei gave her a big hug. "Thank you very much Alexei, for being a friend to my son."

Me, "Don't worry about us mom. Alexei is not gay."

Mom, "You know that doesn't matter to me, as long as you are safe. And make sure you respect Alexei's boundaries. He's been very kind to you."

I just ignored my mom as she went up to bed, and we sat on the couch in front of the T.V. "Alexei come sit down, let me show you this."

Alexei, "I am perfectly happy."

Me, "Huh?"

Alexei, "You told your mom I was not happy."

I then realized I had to explain the birds and the bees
to Alexei, at least that concept of the birds and the bees, and I
did so. Alexei looked a little repulsed.

Alexei, "But that is forbidden in the Bible."

Me, "Yeah, a lot of stuff is forbidden in the Bible, we
really don't care about all that anymore. Anyhow your
government abolished the sex codes in Russia. I'm a little
surprised in your response."

Alexei, "They did? Well, I really was not consulted
about what Mr. Kerensky did or did not do. But the Bible
also says thou without sin shall cast the first stone. Who am I
to judge."

I had always so admired Alexei for the abolition of
the sex codes, but in this moment I realized Alexei had
absolutely nothing to do with the abolishment of the sex
codes. His response seemed a little backwards, but he did at
least concede who is he to judge.

I turned on the T.V. and Alexei looked on with
amazement.

Alexei, "Wow, I always loved film, but this is so much
better with sounds and color, you do not have to read the

subtitles."

I knew Alexei had adored the old silent films. Alexei's Diaries even mentioned "The Mysterious Hand of New York," and how he waited in anticipation to see it. I then asked Alexei, "I have the movie "Tsar Alexei II, the last Tsar of Russia." Want to watch it?"

Alexei, "Boring, let's watch something funny."

I then flicked it to the Simpsons and Married with Children. Alexei's face was far more amusing as he seemed to swing between confusion, amusement, and disgust. Alexei had such an animation to him. Then it was done.

Alexei, "That was sure different."

Me, "I doubt you saw that in 1923, but now please watch Tsar Alexei II with me. I really want your opinion."

Alexei, "If we must."

I then plugged it into the VCR, as Alexei endlessly critiqued how much the actors didn't look like the real people, how it didn't happen that way, how he didn't say it exactly like that. I had always loved the movie, but Alexei did not seem very impressed.

Alexei, "They turned me into a liberal."

Me, "But you are a liberal."

Alexei, just laughed, "I guess you know me better than I know myself. You say you are a student of mine. Do you not remember one of the main lines of my main speech.

"I am not a Bolshevik, I am not a Liberal, I am not a Monarchist. I am not a politician of any kind. I, unlike the rest of them, did not choose to be here. I am here because my family has ruled over this country for over 300 years, some believe we were ordained to rule by God. I am a Russian and so are all of you." or "The politicians argue over ideologies that many do not even understand or have never heard of. We are killing each other over ideology." I am not an ideologue of any kind, the politicians bickered while the people suffered, if it would have been about the people, instead of their egos, we could have saved my country." He looked like he was about to cry.

Me, "I thought you were just politically posturing. You believe in equality, you accepted your position as a Constitutional Monarch under the Kerensky government. Do not blame yourself, you and the Kerensky government didn't ruin Russia, your father and grandfather did. You were different."

Alexei, "I am not blaming myself, I am blaming the politicians, I hold no ill will towards Mr. Kerensky, he did his best, and was almost like a father to me in some ways. But just because I held points in common with the Liberals does not make me one. One thing the Liberals did teach me was to think for myself, and that I did do. Please never disrespect my father again. He also did his best, his duty the way he saw it.

Yeah, I was different, but I still failed to save my people, it did not really matter in the end."

I didn't know what to say, so I pressed play on the movie, it had now ended and was moving into short testimonies from the real-life Sergei, and Kolya as old men in the 1990s as they reflected on Alexei's legacy and how much they loved him.

Alexei then broke down in tears. "They were so loyal to me, I loved them so much, it hurts me so much the pain my death caused them. I just want to hug them tight. I told Sergei he was going to get married and have kids, I wish he would have done so. I wish I was a better friend to them, everything was always all about me, I will never be able to make it up to them."

I didn't know what to say to him. I was speechless, Sergei and Kolya both testified how amazing Alexei was, and how Alexei achieved his goals, how he brought hope to the people, and everyone will love him forever. But in this Alexei could only find tears. Then Alexei went silent and seemed clearly agitated.

Alexei, "This is not heaven, this is hell, it is where I will be punished for eternity for my selfishness. You know James, you really can be a bit of a wet blanket."

I was in utter shock, this was not Alexei the way I pictured him. I wasn't trying to hurt him. I loved him.

Alexei then put on his brave face. "I am sorry my friend, I was unfair to you. Let's just go to bed."

I then took him back up to my room, and he completely stripped in front of me, under garment and all. I gave him my underwear, and he asked for a nightgown. I told him that I just slept in my underwear. He seemed concerned about what if he needed to use the restroom and ran into my mom. I gave him an undershirt and sweat shorts. And we lay down in my bed. If Sergei slept with him, I could sleep with him. I thought about showing him the guest room, but this would be more fun. It wasn't like I was going to molest him or anything. I thought about asking him if he thought Sergei was gay. If Sergei was gay, he sure never admitted to it, but you got to wonder. But I figured I wouldn't push my luck.

Me, "It is great to have you here Alexei." Alexei was already turned over on his other side away from me.

Alexei, "Go to sleep."

I was dumbfounded, he was actually ordering me to go to sleep in my own bed, I know Sergei claimed he would do that, but I never really thought about it.

Me, "This is my bed, I will go to sleep when I want to."

Alexei sat up, and looked at me with the most perplexed look, almost speechless. "But I am your guest. Why does everything have to be a contest with you James. If you would kindly, if it is not too much trouble for you, please go to sleep, I will be eternally grateful." He then laid down, turned back around, clearly ignoring me.

Me, "I'm sorry," but Alexei was silent, he either goes to sleep really quickly or he was ignoring me.

I then turned on my other side and was really still and quiet, as Alexei clearly started snoring, and I knew he was asleep, and I finally dozed off.

Chapter 3

We slept in late, the next morning around 10:00 AM I awoke, I realized it had not all been a dream, there was Alexei sitting up, as perky as ever, as if the last night had never happened.

Alexei, smiling broadly, "I'm so glad you are awake my friend. You were going to take me to the boardwalk today. I'm starved, let's have breakfast."

And in that moment everything felt okay, Alexei's smile filled me with warmth. "Yup, let's go downstairs, I will make you some bacon and eggs."

And down we went, he truly was the brother I always wanted, the best friend I never had, I truly realized in that moment why everyone so loved him.

Alexei, "What about your mom?"

Me, "She is probably already gone."

As I was getting ready to make breakfast the phone rang, it was my mom.

Mom, "James, you know I heard Alexei crying last night, he has been so kind to you, you haven't had a friend in many years, I hope you're being nice to him."

I slammed the phone down.

Alexei, "Who was that?"

Me, "Crank calls."

Alexei, "What is a crank call?"

Me, "Somebody pulling a prank on the phone."

Alexei smiled, "Okay, I get it."

I then served Alexei breakfast, bacon, scrambled eggs, toast, orange juice and coffee. Alexei sure liked him some butter on his toast. Alexei then said, "You're sure a great cook James."

Otherwise, we sat there silent, but content.

I shared my clothes with Alexei, he took my jeans, my blue and white striped polo shirt, and an extra pair of white sneakers. We couldn't have him walking through Santa Cruz in his World War I Russian military uniform. Especially with me, looking like the spitting image of Tsar Alexei. I would never live it down. The jeans were a little short on him, the shoes slightly big, but it worked. We walked out the door and down the street, and Alexei was just filled with wonder. He thought it felt exactly like Livadia, his family's summer home in the Crimea. He conceded maybe he was really in heaven after all. We went by a little clothing store downtown, and got him a good pair of shoes, that actually fit him. His hemophiliac bleeds gave him a slight stiffness in his joints, and he really needed the proper support. He loved the shoes, he felt they were the best shoes he had ever had in his life. We then walked down to the beach and lay in the sand. Alexei decided he was going to bury me alive and sat back to admire his work.

Alexei, "Is there a place with less people, maybe we could strip and go swimming?"

I knew Alexei's love of skinny dipping.

Me, "Not unless you want to end up on the sex offender registry, but I got a pool in my backyard, we can likely get away with it there tonight, if we keep the back lights off."

Alexei looking perplexed again, "What is the sex offender registry?"

And I had to explain to him what sex offenders were and the registry.

Alexei, "That is disgusting. You have people like that here?"

Me, "People like that have always existed, we just address the issue now and don't pretend like it doesn't exist."

Alexei, "But I still don't understand what that has to do with going swimming, what does that have to do with sex?"

Me, "Some consider nudity sexual."

Alexei, "We are guys, you Protestants are so serious."

I just laughed.

Alexei, "Well if we are going to get arrested for going swimming, then I'm ready for you to take me to the boardwalk now."

And with that we went to the boardwalk, Alexei had corn dogs, cotton candy, slushies, and various types of candy, I didn't think he would ever stop eating. We went on the roller coaster and Alexei screamed his head off. He was so much fun to watch. Then we went inside, and I showed him the video games, he was truly enthralled.

As we went by the bowling alley it happened. There was a group of assholes from my high school. And Alexei just wandered on up to them clearly enthralled in the game. But it wasn't as I expected. Alexei seemed sincerely curious in their sport and complimented them much on their skill. When they let Alexei have a try, Alexei completely bombed it. Alexei broke out laughing, joking about how unathletic he was. His accent seemed to interest them, and he explained how his name was Alexei, he was visiting from Russia, and his grandmother was English, and his mother raised them in English, while his dad spoke Russian. They seemed truly engrossed in him. I just didn't get it. Alexei wasn't cool, Alexei was warm, Alexei was a bit of a dork, and a klutz. Why did they like him. Of course, they just had to invite him to their party that night, and then it happened. He pointed back towards me.

Alexei, "Can I bring my friend James?"

Matt, "You're from Russia, your name is Alexei, and you're hanging out with James?"

They all broke out laughing hysterically, Alexei clearly didn't get it, but chuckled along.

Dan, "Yeah bring him, we need someone to dunk in the pool."

Alexei, just laughed, "Toss me in the pool if you want, that sounds like fun, thanks for letting me bring James, he is a good guy if you get to know him."

Alan, "Yeah we know James," smirking, he then waved at me, "Looking forward to seeing you tonight, James, bring your bathing suit, or don't."

I just stood there, glaring at the assholes with complete contempt, if they were not stronger than me, I would have knocked them senseless.

Alexei then walked towards me smiling and waving back at them and put his arm around my shoulder, and whispered in my ear, "Smile and wave back at them now."

Me, "No."

And we walked off in silence. As we were clear out of distance, Alexei said to me, "You really wonder why you don't have any friends?"

Me, "They are complete assholes, they even told you, they are going to throw me in the pool, they're not joking, they will throw me in the pool if we go to that party. I have no clue why they were nice to you, maybe you're just an oddity."

Alexei, "They seemed like good guys. Why do you care If they throw you in the pool? You don't like to swim? The boys and I used to toss each other in the pond back at the Alexander Palace."

Me, "That was different."

Alexei, "Why?"

Me, "You're such a nice guy, and they're assholes."

Alexei, "Well I guess we will see at the party tonight."

Me, "We're not going."

Alexei, "Yes we are."

Me, "No we're not."

Alexei, "Well I guess we could just hang around your place and play with your dolls," as he gave me a friendly shove, then put his arm back around my shoulder smiling.

I loved Alexei, but sometimes I didn't know what to make of him. He was really not cool, but why did they like him? He seemed to have my peers dialed in more than me. I just smiled, it did feel good to have a friend. We went out and laid on the beach a while longer, and Alexei kept joking about how we just need to strip and go swimming, that maybe it would be fun to get arrested, how could they arrest the Tsar of all Russia. I told him that unless he wanted to end up getting 5150ed, or end up the subject of government experiments, he might want to keep that to himself. We walked up through the quaint early 20th century downtown

with the big old trees and had ice cream, though Alexei had
ice cream before, all the different flavors shocked him, then
we walked home and watched T.V.

Chapter 4

As it was getting later, I was dreading, as I knew Alexei was going to start harassing me to go to that party. Alexei always had to get his way. My mother walked in the door with McDonald's for the three of us, she obviously sensed Alexei was still here, and Alexei was his usual charming self. He loved the big mac, fries and coke, and of course my mom had to be irritating.

Mom, "I hope James is being nice to you Alexei, James could so use a friend."

I rolled my eyes.

Alexei, "James is a great friend, I could not hope for a better friend."

Mom, "You are too kind."

Alexei, "No you and James are too kind to graciously host me in your home."

My mom just chuckled.

Alexei, "James is going to kindly take me to a party tonight, I look so forward to getting to know the other guys."

Me, "No I'm not."

Mom, "Yes you are, Alexei is your guest, anyhow it will do you some good, maybe Alexei can teach you a thing or two."

I just sighed as Alexei smiled at me. Alexei could be

annoying, but I just couldn't hate him. There was just that something about him that made you want to love him. And so after dinner we walked to the party. Alexei mentioned he had a coke before, but it tasted different, and he had fries on occasion before, but they seemed different, but Alexei clearly had never had a hamburger. Alexei mused it was too bad he wouldn't have the time to introduce hamburgers to Russia once he returned. It sent shivers down my spine. How could Alexei want to return to be assassinated. I wanted him to stay here with me, forever. I mean what harm would it cause? The timeline had not been disrupted, and Alexei could live. But I put the thought out of my mind, and I figured I would cross that bridge when I came to it.

We entered the backyard of this very large house, the family was obviously richer than mine, there was liquor and marijuana, and everyone was having a good time, but me. These were the cool kids, I felt so out of place. But everyone was curious about Alexei the visitor from Russia. He wasn't cool, but his charm was apparently timeless. Alexei had a beer and smoked pot, very clearly enjoying himself. The girls were very warm to him as well. Alexei wasn't just going to be best friends with the assholes, he was going to get the girl as well. I always envisioned Alexei to be a little more like me. As I saw him, I didn't want anyone to hurt him, but I felt a tinge of jealousy. I wanted to get us tossed out, I wanted to teach

Alexei a lesson, and then in the most mocking voice I could, I told the jocks from earlier.

"Looks like Alexei is moving in on your girls," as I laughed like a maniac.

Matt, "Who cares, you jealous James?"

Dan, "I think it is time for you to take that dunk," he grabbed me getting ready to throw me in the pool.

Alexei quickly got up coming over, "Hey boys, is everything good?"

Alan, "Your friend here was trying to get us to kick your ass, but we thought, it was time for him to chill out in the pool a bit."

Alexei, "Then let me do the honors," as Alexei grabbed me and tossed me in the pool. Alexei then jumped in the pool with me, "Hey guys, this is fun, come on in," and several of them actually jumped in fully clothed and all started splashing each other. Alexei turned to me smiling, "It was me or them." And I just smiled, how could I hate Alexei.

We got out and Alexei got back to this one pretty blonde girl who seemed particularly into him. They disappeared for a little while, whatever they did, I will never know, but Alexei came back with quite a look of accomplishment on his face. Alexei ended up coming back and sitting with me a bit as we chilled. And some guy, obviously drunk and stoned came walking up to us and told

Alexei to get up. Alexei got up smiling, that look of friendship on his face.

Eric, "You just waltz in here from Russia, thinking you're so cool."

Alexei, "Huh," with that perplexed look on his face, and then Eric shoved Alexei, as Alexei fell back hitting the ground.

I was so scared in that moment that he had hurt Alexei, they didn't know that this was the hemophiliac last Tsar of Russia. Some of the other boys came running up, holding him back.

Matt, "What is wrong with you, if you're going to act like that get out of my party."

Alexei then got up, with a more serious look on his face, "It is fine, we were just playing around, do not throw him out."

Matt, "If you say so."

The guy who had pushed Alexei then just glared at Alexei and walked off.

As we walked home in the early morning hours, Alexei clearly had the time of his life. He was clearly surprised to see unchaperoned girls, he thought the party was going to be all guys, or a chaperoned party, he clearly had never experienced anything like it. He then said to me in a serious tone.

Alexei, "Somebody told me you dumped some kid out of a wheelchair?"

In that moment I felt embarrassed, I knew Alexei had often been in a wheelchair at times due to the pain and disability of his hemophiliac bleeds. That wasn't something I would normally do. That incident was a few years ago, I couldn't believe the assholes were still talking about that.

Me, "You don't understand, they are warping it, I would have never tossed you out of your wheelchair, you're such a good guy, that kid was making fun of me. Even the retards make fun of me."

Alexei, "Just because someone is in a wheelchair does not make them retarded. I spent many times confined to one. But if he's retarded as you say, he clearly has more problems than you. Sometimes you have to stop just thinking about yourself."

Alexei then lightened up, "Thank you so much for taking me tonight, it was so much fun, never experienced anything like that in my life. I was only allowed a small group of handpicked friends."

When we got home, I indulged Alexei, we took our clothes off in my backyard, with the lights out, and went skinny dipping in my pool. The party was kind of interesting, but it was my time alone with Alexei I treasured, as we rough housed in the pool. We then went up to my room and went to bed, not getting up until 3:00 the next afternoon.

Chapter 5

And so it went on for several weeks, we would hang out at the beach, or the boardwalk, often have dinner with mom, watch movies, go skinny dipping in the pool. Alexei liked board and card games and we would occasionally play them if we got bored enough. Alexei and I would play chess, he was one hell of a chess player. But Alexei often preferred the stuff he couldn't do in his time, the color films with sound, and the amusements of the boardwalk. I made breakfast and we often bought lunch. I made Alexei my famous dip of mixed condiments, herbs, and spices for the frozen fried clams and fries. Alexei was polite but didn't seem to be a fan. But otherwise, Alexei would compliment my cooking skills.

Alexei was getting invited to all the parties. This was our last summer before college and there were a lot of them, the last hurrah. I went with Alexei, I wasn't the center of attention, but I was pleasantly surprised, as I kept a low profile and people largely left me alone. Alexei's nemesis from the first party clearly was not a fan, but in Alexei's popularity, the guy pretty much decided to leave Alexei alone. Alexei tried his best to pull me into the fun, and at times it was a little fun. It was a different experience for me. Yeah, some of them were jerks, but maybe they weren't all as bad as

I thought. Matt especially was a tease but could also be quite caring. But everyone sure loved Alexei.

We spent little time on Russian history, Alexei didn't seem to enjoy it. But he did agree to go over my book of his pictures with me, on the condition that he wouldn't see any pictures of his shooting or the aftermath. The big book I had stopped with him standing on the platform speaking in Ekaterinburg anyway. Alexei took great joy as we went over his youth, his years of unofficial house arrest under the Kerensky government, and his final standing up to Kerensky, the speech at the Winter Palace, his final reunion with his family in Livadia, and then his fateful train tour.

But Alexei didn't spend a lot of time on the politics of it, he seemed far more interested in the relationships and the odd quirks of the people in his life. Alexei had some very amusing tales of his antics as a little boy. He was just adorable in his sailor's outfit and with his donkey Vanka. And you could feel the empathy he felt for the soldiers during his time with his dad at the front. Alexei clearly respected his father though gently acknowledged he would not have made all the same decisions. Alexei also respected that Nicholas in the end treated him as a man and respected his autonomy, even if Nicholas had not agreed with him. You could feel Alexei's love for his family, friends, and staff.

I found his relationship with Alexander Kerensky

fascinating, how Kerensky abducted him, controlled him, and attempted to manipulate him, but that Alexei also to some degree felt him as a father-like figure. I never truly realized how he had zero influence over the government. Only in those final months after Alexei stood up to Kerensky, was Alexei truly doing Alexei, but even then, though Kerensky humored the role Alexei decided to play as a figurehead, otherwise the politicians had completely ignored him. It was in the Russian people that Alexei truly found himself and he truly enjoyed. He seemed to most enjoy his stops off the beaten path, his engagement with the Jewish community in Minsk, and the poor peasant village outside of Moscow. It was in these engagements he felt he really got to know the real Russia. Then we came to him in Ekaterinburg, which he did not recognize, but the place and date became pretty clear to him. Without a word he quickly went back to some of his childhood favorites. I politely listened and asked him an occasional gentle question. I didn't argue with him or insert my thoughts into his life.

There was a simplicity to him. This young man born to be Tsar, but who did not seem to care for politics or political ideology. He was very intelligent, but his prism of the world was an emotional one. While I fell in love with the myth, in the end I loved the man even more. Sergei once said that the myth cannot capture the magic of being in the presence of the live Alexei, and in that he was right. I asked Alexei to sign the book and he did, I figured nobody would know it was really Alexei's.

As Alexei and I were lying in bed one night, I was thinking, then asked Alexei, "I will be in college in the fall, and my parents will pay for a big summer trip for me. Want to go to Russia? It would be so much fun."

Alexei, "Boring."

Me, "Why? You were the Tsar of Russia, wouldn't you like to see it now, the Communists have fallen, it is a new age."

Alexei, "I've been to Russia, anyhow don't you think me haunting the Alexander Palace might creep people out. I would prefer to go to New York, I always wanted to see New York, I remember seeing the "Mysterious Hand of New York" as a kid, I always waited in anticipation for the next segment to come out. If you take me to New York, I would be forever grateful."

I sighed, "Okay we will go to New York."

My father came home to drive us to the San Francisco Airport, I hadn't seen him in weeks. He was his usual self, caught up in his own affairs. As we were packing, Alexei packed his army suit, I wasn't sure why he would be needing it, unless he was planning a career in playing Tsar Alexei on Broadway or something. That might be kind of creepy if he got much attention, as everyone couldn't get quite past how he is the spitting image of Alexei. He also insisted we bring the time travel wand. As we got in the car, my father asked Alexei to ride up front, that he had heard about him from my mom, but had not really gotten to meet him. I sat in the back.

Dad, "So Alexei, my wife tells me you're quite the amazing young man, and you have been quite the amazing influence on James."

Alexei, "Thank you for your kind words, sir, but it is James that has been such a great friend to me."

My dad kind of chuckled, "I think you've probably figured out by now James doesn't really have friends."

I just sat there in silence, as I knew my father was preparing to humiliate me, I knew talking back to him did no good, and I didn't want him to refuse to pay for our trip. I figured Alexei would have his way with him, like he did everyone.

Alexei, "I wouldn't know, but James gets along great with me, and he has been getting along great with the guys at the parties we have gone to. I do really want to thank you sir and your wife for hosting me, it has been such a fun time."

Dad, "My wife says you're straight."

Alexei looked perplexed, and I figured I probably needed to help him out.

Me, "Alexei isn't gay, he has gotten on quite well with the girls at the parties."

Dad, "Alexei is a very well-spoken young man, I think he can answer for himself."

Alexei, "Yes sir, I didn't quite realize what straight meant to Americans, but yes, I'm straight, I'm not gay."

Dad, "Maybe you can toughen James up a bit, he could sure use it."

I rolled my eyes.

Alexei, "In my observations James is quite tough, but I will do what I can sir."

Dad, "You Russian boys are sure polite, these American kids these days are spoiled rotten."

Alexei, "Thank you sir, my parents always taught me the importance of politeness."

Dad, "Give my regards to them for a job well done, you know your name being Alexei, you being some rich kid from Russia, the spitting image of the last Tsar, my wife says you were even doing Alexei in a play when you showed up and were fully uniformed, I'm sure that is what drew James to you. But I'm glad it did. James always needed a friend, and it seems you have been good for him."

Alexei, "Thank you for your kindness."

Dad, "I've seen Tsar Alexei in all James's pictures, you really are the spitting image of him, a little spooky, I would think you were a reincarnation if I didn't know better. My wife says you're only a distant cousin."

Alexei, "Yes, to my knowledge sir."

Dad, "Well you see look a likes, James has always been obsessed with Tsar Alexei."

Alexei chuckled, looking back at me, "Yes I've gotten to know that."

Then my dad just bantered on with Alexei about his life in Russia and what Alexei thought of America. Alexei loved America, my dad thought Russia sounded a little quaint, but he guessed they are not as wealthy as Americans. Alexei acknowledged his extreme privilege, and the poverty many Russians were in. And like my mom, my dad thought Alexei would be President of Russia someday. Alexei, as always, did manage, his slip ups were slight and explainable, and in his charm my dad didn't really care. I think he would have adopted Alexei if he could, and I am sure Alexei would have been his favorite son. But what did I care, in the end my dad always tried to make up for his disinterest in me with his money, and if I was going to get to spend my summer with his money, and Alexei, I figured I would just smile and bear it.

We entered the San Francisco airport, this was the first time Alexei had ever seen an airport before, and he was clearly awe struck. Alexei had the passport I had bought carefully forged for him. We were rich, English speaking, clean cut, white boys, no one was going to pay close attention. And we had the time travel charm if things went wrong. I figured this was easier than explaining to my parents us beaming to New York where their credit cards suddenly become active. As we sat on the plane, Alexei mentioned he had seen early planes a few times, but nothing like this, and Alexei of course got the window seat. But I was fine just sitting next to my dear sweet Alexei.

Chapter 6

Coming into New York, looking at the skyline, it looked like Alexei was going to pop out of his seat. In this moment I was glad I had brought Alexei to New York. We did everything, we went out to the Statue of Liberty and to the top of the World Trade Center. We caught a play, I wanted to see a play on Alexei, but Alexei wanted to see something funny, and as usual Alexei won. We found some old school slapstick and Alexei's laughter filled the theater, as everyone was looking at us.

We were in the food capital of the world, but Alexei wanted hamburgers and hot dogs, he couldn't get enough of them. He entertained me with a Russian restaurant. Alexei said it was similar, but not quite what he remembered. We went to the museums and Alexei quite enjoyed the fine art. And Alexei just adored Central Park, he said parts of it slightly reminded him of the grounds of the Alexander Palace. But what Alexei enjoyed most of all was Coney Island and we did it all, the roller coaster, the ferris wheel, the games and Alexei was quite good at some of them, but told them to keep the prizes, he wouldn't need them. Alexei could not get enough of the corn dogs, cotton candy, and all the various kinds of candy available in the modern age. Then we went out and laid on the beach.

Alexei, "You know James, I think we should go skinny dipping."

I gave him that look like it wasn't going to happen.

Alexei, "Just pranking you James," as he chuckled.

We both smiled. I wished this summer could go on for eternity.

Our hotel was overlooking Times Square, and we laid back in bed one night.

Me, "I'm sorry for how embarrassing my father was."

Alexei, "It was fine, he wouldn't have been asking me those questions if he didn't care about you."

Me, "He has never been that interested in me, he is always working, he buys me off with money, but I guess that has its advantages, here we are."

Alexei sympathetically, "It can be tough, being away from your family, when I was a kid and I was away at the front with Papa, I missed Mama. When I was at the Alexander Palace with Mama and Papa was at the front, I missed him. And when Kerensky abducted me for over six years, I was allowed no contact with my family, my previous friends, my tutors, my assistants, they were all taken from me. I only got a final few weeks with them after I made clear to Mr. Kerensky I was going to do what I wanted, and the only way he was going to stop me was to hurt me."

Me, "But your parents so loved and adored you, and

your sisters, and your staff, tutors and friends, you had so much love. And even after you were abducted, you had Sergei, and your cook, and maid, and Mr. Kerensky brought by his sons and the sons of some of the other Duma members to keep you company. And you got to see Dr. Derevenko on occasion and pass letters to Kolya. I always dreamed I was there with you and Sergei, under house arrest at the Alexander Palace. The silent movies, swimming to the island, the snowball fights, the games, playing with your pets, just hanging out on the grounds. I have dreamed it for so much of my life."

Alexei, "I admit, I have had so much love in my life, and for that I am eternally grateful for everyone who has been a part of it. But I have had pain. Sometimes my hemophiliac bleeds were so painful, I just wanted to die so the pain would stop. I think that might have helped bring my family together and allowed us to cherish the time we had, because quite often we all thought I was going to die. I'm grateful for my friends, but I had never been allowed more than a few hand-picked friends. My parents didn't usually let me play with my cousins for fear they might hurt me and only allowed a few sons of staff members to regularly spend time with me. Same with Mr. Kerensky, bringing his sons and the sons of other Duma members to influence me. I was rarely allowed out of the Alexander Palace during house arrest. I was trapped in the gilded cage. And even in my last few months of freedom, I was under constant threat of assassination and had the guards always traipsing after me. And apparently I was assassinated weeks short of my 19th birthday, devastating my family and friends, while my country drowned in blood. Your parents obviously care for you, and what you have is freedom, to go where you want, to do what you want, to hang out with whom you want, without fear of being murdered, in a very rich country at peace. And you have your whole life ahead of you. Do not envy me, it is I who envy you."

Me, "But you admit, you had so much love, I'm so alone, I have never had anyone, you're my only friend, you're the only person I have ever really cared about."

Alexei, "Maybe if you gave others in your life, the love you have given me, you wouldn't be alone."

We just laid there in silence, I couldn't imagine giving others the love I had given Alexei. Alexei was just such an amazing human being. And for once, Alexei didn't order me to go to sleep.

While in New York, Alexei was determined that we were going to a Russian Orthodox Service and that he was going to receive confession and communion. I told him I was not sure if I should attend as I was not Russian Orthodox. Alexei asked me what I was, and I told him I didn't really know. Then Alexei insisted I was going to go to Church with him and how much it would mean to him. And so I did. The Church was impressive, it was covered in carvings, paintings of saints and angels, the ceiling was very high, and the wooden paneling behind the altar with its colorful paintings stood out. Alexei was confessed. The prayers, and the reading of scripture were interesting, it all had so much feeling. Alexei received the Eucharist. And the Priest commented on how Alexei was the spitting image of Tsar Alexei. Alexei said I should attend Orthodox service more often, that it would provide me comfort and I wouldn't feel so alone.

Me, "You know, there would be no better way to convert me to the Russian Orthodox faith, than for us to go to Russia."

Alexei smiled, "I have another place in mind. You know the most sacred Orthodox Church is in Jerusalem?"

Me, "Jerusalem?"

Alexei, "I have always wanted to see the Holy Land, you wouldn't deny me the opportunity to commune with Our Lord and Savior, would you?"

Me, "Well, I guess, hopefully my parents will not mind."

Alexei, "You just offered to take me to Russia, if we can go to Russia, I see no reason we can't go to Jerusalem instead."

Me, "Okay."

Alexei, "You're the bestest friend a Tsar ever had!" And Alexei smiled his famous smile, and then he said in a more serious tone, "You know it will be sad to leave New York, this could very well be heaven, but I'm looking very forward to the Holy Land. Maybe you will convert. There is no better place, than where Christ gave himself so we could live."

Me, "You know, I would enjoy anywhere with you." And Alexei once again flashed his famous smile.

Then pretty quickly we were on the plane to Jerusalem so Alexei could commune with Christ. And as usual Alexei got the window seat. In the words of Alexei, he was my guest after all. How could I deny him, and this was all so new to him.

Chapter 7

We landed in Tel-Aviv. Alexei was kind of surprised he had never heard of Tel-Aviv in the land he knew as Palestine. I had to explain to him the Jews had in fact returned to Zion and created the State of Israel. Alexei seemed happy they had found a homeland but was curious about the native Palestinians. As I explained the current state of affairs, he seemed saddened.

Alexei, "We have both Jewish and Muslim citizens in Russia, and we had peace for many years, I don't see why they cannot live together in peace in Palestine."

I was not sure how peacefully the Jews or Muslims had lived in Russia, but I wasn't going to argue with Alexei. We enjoyed the city of Tel-Aviv for a day or two, Alexei felt it reminded him of Livadia. Alexei found his love of falafel gyros, and since the drinking age is 18, we had a cocktail or two, he liked the sweet ones. Alexei was determined we would start in Bethlehem then go to Egypt, I think Alexei wanted an excuse to see the pyramids, then up to Galilee, then to Jerusalem even though this logistically made no sense. And so, we went on Alexei's journey in the footsteps of Christ.

Much of Bethlehem is made of old beige stones. It is quite hilly and feels really old. We of course went to see the

Church of the Nativity. You felt this ancient presence beyond yourself, then we ventured down into the crypt or the cave where Christ was born. Alexei, normally quite jovial, was in a very serious mood. You could tell he felt touched by an outer presence. His golden crucifix he normally wore under his clothes was out and he was gripping it tight. I stood there in silence as Alexei contemplated Christ. We also visited the Milk Grotto where Jesus and his family hid after Herod ordered his death, before they were able to flee to Egypt. And then off to Egypt we were.

In Egypt the main thing we did was go to the Pyramids at Giza and saw the Sphinx. Alexei with that smile on his face had that look of awe.

Me, "This is cool, but not sure what it has to do with Christ."

Alexei chuckled, "Well if Jesus was in Egypt, he must have seen the pyramids."

We got up close to the sphinx wandering around it.

Alexei, "Don't you think it looks like a lion?"

Me, "Yeah kind of."

Alexei, "You know it was buried in sand at one time up to its neck. Napoleon's army blew off its nose. Tsar Alexander I taught Napoleon a lesson, it was Alexander who finally sent him packing back to France."

Apparently, Alexei knew his history. Then we climbed

the large pyramid. It was a bit of a struggle for Alexei, but as we sat on the top, Alexei was out of breath and looking like he was in slight pain, but I could tell Alexei felt it was worth it. He just looked in awe over the Nile Delta and the desert. We sat there for hours, and Alexei finally said.

Alexei, "This world is so beautiful, so fun, so splendid, this feels like the last temptation of Christ. You do not know how lucky you are James."

I wasn't sure what Alexei meant by the last temptation of Christ, so I just volunteered. "This is pretty amazing and even more amazing with you here sitting next to me."

Alexei gave me that contemplative look and looked like he was about to say something, but then he just turned his head back out and looked in silence, we watched the sunset, then night fell, and we looked at the stars and the full moon.

Alexei, "You think heaven is on one of those stars James, that our ancestors are just watching over us, knowing the cosmic plan with a sense of peace?"

Me, "Maybe, I think you would know more about heaven than me."

Alexei, "I am thinking more of my great grandfather Alexander II these days, I have always admired him, he freed the serfs, but they still killed him. I hope to see him in heaven. Papa always said he was a jovial guy."

Me, "But you're here with me, we have the rest of our lives ahead of us."

Alexei gave me that peering look once again, but then just laughed and smiled. We watched the sun come up, and the next morning we came down. They were shocked we were still here. We took a cab back to Cairo and slept the entire day. That night we enjoyed some of the Cairo nightlife. Technically the drinking age is 21 but no one checks. Alexei ended up running into some Russians, who he had some fun with. He told them he was Tsar Alexei II. They just laughed. He then regaled them with tales of his life which they found very entertaining and told him he was an excellent actor. But they admitted they could see the resemblance.

Before we left Cairo and went back on the Jesus trail Alexei wanted to visit a Mosque, he had never made it to visit Russia's Muslim subjects and was quite interested. He asked the Imam many questions which were answered in broken English. Alexei apologized he had never gotten around to learning Arabic, but the Imam seemed delighted in Alexei's polite curiosity. In the end Alexei said "Jews, Christians, Muslims, we are all the children of Abraham, we are all the children of God."

And then we zipped up to Galilee where Jesus grew up. Galilee is greener than what we had seen so far, with lots of sparse pine-looking trees, it was almost as if you were in the hills of California. We visited Nazareth village where we saw how it would have looked at the time of Christ. The little stone huts, the vegetable plots, the olive trees, the sheep and donkeys, the actors dressed in the garb of the time, it really immersed you in the experience, almost like Jesus would come sprinting around the corner. I dare not go back in time and collect him, disrupting the cosmic plan of God, I wasn't sure if I believed, but well just in case.

Alexei was having the time of his life and in a particularly lighthearted mood. Seeing Jesus's childhood seemed to make Alexei think of his own childhood and I always loved hearing Alexei tell the tales of his youth. When he got up in the early morning on the family yacht and ordered the royal band to play, when he stole a dinner guest's shoe, and when his father told him to put it back, he put a strawberry in it, how he enjoyed walking back and forth in front of the guards to be saluted until his father ordered them to stop saluting Alexei, when he threw some lady's parasol in the pond, but after his father chastised him that was no way to treat a lady, he felt so bad and profusely apologized. He would have been such a fun playmate as a kid. I never wanted this to end.

But then it was on to the grand finale, Jerusalem. We stayed at the King David Hotel just outside The Old City.

The pink limestone building feels like a cross between ancient Jerusalem and the Art Deco style of the 1930s. But we spent very little time in it, as we spent most of our time exploring the Old City. This was like Bethlehem on steroids. The ancient beige stone buildings were just huge, and you were sucked back in time. The Old City behind giant old stonewalls has a Muslim Quarter, Christian Quarter, Jewish Quarter and Armenian Quarter. There is the Temple Mount, which is the site of the Jewish Wailing Wall, a part of the Second Temple, and on top of it sits the Al Aqsa Mosque, the site from which Muslims believe Mohammed after being carried to Jerusalem by a winged horse ascended into heaven. Alexei felt this community with its diversity was proof the children of Abraham could live together in peace.

The Church of the Holy Sepulcher believed to be on top of the original crucifixion and burial spots of Christ was certainly the highlight for Alexei. It looked kind of like a medieval castle with a large blue dome. Alexei took Greek Orthodox service in the main Chapel as I sat beside him. The Greeks represent the Orthodox community at the Church.

As it ended, Alexei turned to me, "I know you want Jesus in your heart. You will never be lonely again."

Me, "All I need is you."

Alexei smiled and with a bit of sarcasm in his voice, "Well you are on the right track, but I am not the Son of

God."

We then headed to the spot of Calvary where Jesus was crucified. You could see Jesus hanging on the crucifix propped up by a wooden altar, with a golden half sun like stand behind it. Alexei was in a very serious mood as he contemplated the crucifixion.

Alexei then turned to me, "Have I ever told you the story of the crucifixion of St. Peter?"

Me, "Nope."

Alexei, "Peter upon hearing that he was to be crucified, fled Rome to save his life, but on that road, he ran into Jesus walking towards Rome. Peter of course was excited to see Jesus again but asked Jesus what he was doing. Jesus replied that he was heading to Rome to be crucified again. With that Peter felt great shame and returned to Rome to be crucified."

Me, "Wow, who would do that."

Alexei, "If Jesus went to the cross so we could live, who was Peter to run away from his fate. We must try to have the courage to do what is right."

I felt a shiver down my spine, but Alexei just had that sense of serene calm.

As we were walking out of the Church, I once again said, "This has been a lot of fun, but if you really want to convert me to Russian Orthodoxy, there is no place to do it like Russia."

Alexei, "I was thinking Japan."

Me, "What does Japan have to do with Christ or Russian Orthodoxy?"

Alexei, "Nothing, I just always wanted to see Japan, Papa went there once and it sounded so different, I always imagined what it would be like. If you take me to Japan, then I will accompany you to Russia."

Me, "Well I guess, but I think I have gone through my vacation funds for the next several years."

Alexei, "Well you get to do this with me, you say you treasure our time together. We may never have another opportunity. Let's make the most of it."

Chapter 8

And then like that we were off to Japan with Alexei at the window. We landed in Tokyo. I had imagined Tokyo being a land of cherry blossoms and pagodas, but Tokyo is much more like New York with its skyscrapers, but is also different, with plenty of brightly colored buildings and huge neon signs. Tokyo was a bit surreal. Alexei wasn't a fan of sushi but found his love of tempura, teppanyaki, and plenty of sake.

Alexei always knew how to strike up a conversation with anyone who spoke English, or Russian, or French. When hanging out with other young people at night in the izakayas, a bar with snacks, Alexei liked to introduce himself to people as Tsar Alexei and tell stories of his life. Alexei had great fun, but little did his listeners know he wasn't pulling their leg. Alexei had this magical charm to him, he really could draw about anyone to him. Since the legal drinking age was 20, we couldn't get into the clubs, but the restaurants and izakayas were more lax.

Alexei was having great fun, but also wanted to see the historical Japan, the Japan his father would have seen. I was having fun but looking forward to Russia, unless Alexei wanted me to take him to Timbuktu next. But Alexei said we would go to Russia, and I believed him. When Alexei learned of the atom bombs that had been dropped on Japan, I sensed a sadness, and he turned towards me wondering where the honor was in that.

Then we went to Kyoto the old imperial capital and the cultural hub of old Japan, this was the Japan of pagodas and cherry blossoms, old wooden buildings, weeping willows and bonsai. Alexei was in a trance, he truly loved it. We saw Nijo Castle the old wooden and paper palace of the old Japanese Emperors. Alexei was fascinated by the Samurai and Ninja Museum. We looked at the strange produce in the market and Alexei just adored the monkey park, as he laughed at their antics. He lamented he never had a monkey as a child and wondered how the Tsesarevich of Russia could have been deprived of a monkey. He just knew there had to be monkeys in heaven. I felt like I could watch Alexei watching the monkeys forever.

But then once again Alexei was on his search for God as we visited the Shinto Shrines and Buddhist Temples and boy does Kyoto have a lot of them. The Kiyomizu Buddhist Temple was amazing, with its elaborate red and white pagoda gates with the elaborate wooden buildings behind them. And the golden statue of a standing Kannon the goddess of mercy. The Shinto Fushimi Shrine was largely of polished cherry looking wood, with Japanese characters on it. Shintoism sees God in nature, sees God all around.

As we were leaving Alexei looked towards me with a serious look in his eye, "You know James, my path to God is through Christ, but it is all God."

I just pondered a bit, "You know, I've never thought much about God, but in getting to know you and see your true faith, I may just come to believe."

Alexei, smiling, "I'm glad to hear that. I really want to thank you so much for everything you have done for me. You're a good guy James, don't let anyone tell you any different. You truly are the bestest friend a Tsar ever had."

I smiled, "I love being with you, I'm happier than I have ever been."

Alexei stared off a bit, as if lost in his thoughts.

We stayed a few more days in Kyoto, I don't think Alexei ever wanted to leave, it was almost as if he could have stayed here forever. Alexei mused he would like to get a tattoo like his dad, but it might be hard to explain since in his timeline he had never been to Japan. Alexei had to go to the monkey park one final time, and on our last night we had an amazing teppanyaki and plum wine. Alexei truly loved plum wine.

Alexei, "I'm all yours now, we will go to Russia, as you wish. I'm ready to haunt the Alexander Palace," he said with a laugh.

I was looking so forward to our trip to Russia, and

with Tsar Alexei II. This was unbelievable. As we were getting on the plane, I could feel Alexei growing somber. He told me to take the window seat which kind of surprised me. He then tilted his head back and looked up deep in thought. His eyes were watery as if he was going to cry. I all a suddenly felt bad. I didn't see how he could not want to go to Russia, he had been the Tsar of. But after about 30 minutes or so, Alexei snapped out of it and began making friends with the other passengers. I never quite understood, how he could bounce out of his moods so quickly, but we were on our way to St. Petersburg, and I hoped this would be the Alexei I would see Russia with.

Chapter 9

As we came in the airport, we saw the picture of the former president Boris Yeltsin and I mentioned to Alexei how Gorbachev and Yeltsin had brought a new freedom to Russia, and as Russia contemplated its future, Alexei's legacy had seen a resurgence, as people debated what Alexei would have done, what Alexei would have wanted for Russia. Then we saw the picture of the new president Vladimir Putin. I mentioned to Alexei that Putin, like all politicians, paid homage to the memory of Alexei, but not much was known about him, everyone wondered what this new guy would do. Would he implement Alexei's vision for Russia?

As we rode through St. Petersburg to our hotel, Alexei remarked how much of the historical city was similar, but it was also different. That he kind of liked the old St. Petersburg better. We went to the Church of the Savior on the Spilled Blood where Alexei's great grandfather Alexander II had been assassinated. Alexei admired him and you could tell he was in a contemplative mood. Then we went to see the Winter Palace, and the Hermitage Museum. Alexei was surprised it was blue, and not red the way he remembered it. We saw the room that Alexei was locked with Sergei in during Alexei's first few months as Tsar.

Alexei turning to me, "You know I really never

wanted to see this room again, the first few months were the hardest. I agreed to cooperate because Kerensky made clear to me it was needed for peace, and I made clear to Kerensky my only condition was he protect my family. I feared if soldiers could take me against my will, what they were going to do to my father. They said I was Tsar, but I was clearly the prisoner of the Provisional Government. I really didn't know what they were going to do to me, to my family, and I was so alone."

Me, "But you had Sergei, I always thought this sounded kind of fun, you and him just getting to hang out, and I will not disrespect your father, but the Provisional Government was trying to save Russia."

Alexei, "Now you know, it was not as romantic as you thought it was. Sergei was such a great comfort to me, and we tried to make the best of it. I realize now that the Provisional Government wasn't all bad, but I had no way of knowing their intentions."

I felt both fascinated and sad hearing Alexei's take on it all. I had never really thought about it quite that way before.

Alexei, "Kerensky lightened up after I gave myself the nosebleed."

Me, "You gave yourself the nosebleed?"

Alexei smiling at me, "Yup, my bleeds had brought people closer to me before, I figured at the very least

Kerensky had to let me see Dr. Derevenko. By that point it felt clear that Kerensky wanted me alive. It worked quite well."

Me, "But Sergei said blood was on your pillow and night gown."

Alexei grinning from ear to ear, "It had to look realistic, I went to bed after I did so, then I got up again and woke up Sergei."

I just smiled back at Alexei, I realized even at 12 years old he could be quite manipulative.

Then we went and saw the art exhibits, this was possibly the largest art collection in the world and has a lot of Rembrandts. This was clearly the highlight of Alexei's trip to Russia as he felt like the Alexei I knew. Alexei recognized some of the paintings.

Alexei, "This art collection is even better than the museum in New York."

I just smiled, "I guess you Russians can do something right."

We hung out in St. Petersburg a night or two, and of course Alexei had to do his Tsar Alexei routine on the Russians. As always people were quite entertained and did note the resemblance.

Then we headed up to Pushkin or as Alexei remembered it Tsarskoye Selo for the Alexander Palace, the place I had dreamed of seeing for so long. On our way through Pushkin, Alexei noted some things were similar, but a lot of the buildings were newer. We went to the World War I Museum. Alexei was very serious.

Alexei, "I was dressed in sailor outfits and then after my father took command of the Army, I was switched to the army uniform. Russia was an Empire, and the son of a Tsar was brought up playing war games. The much more powerful Austria Hungary attacked our little brother Serbia, we had to defend them, we had to stand up to the bully. I very much admired the Russian army, and so enjoyed hanging out with the generals, the soldiers, and the cadets at military headquarters. It was the time of my life. But the profound suffering caused by the war, seeing the wounded, also broke my heart. We must work harder for peace."

I just pondered Alexei's thoughts, I really didn't have anything to add. This was the trip I had so wanted, and it was priceless hearing Alexei's thoughts on his experiences, but in some ways, I enjoyed Alexei's trips more, Alexei was having so much fun. This Alexei, though you could tell was trying to remain upbeat, seemed more subdued.

Then it was finally time, we headed up to the Alexander Palace, both Alexei's home and the place I had dreamed about for so long. The grounds and the palace are largely untouched by time, almost like taking a time machine back to Alexei's time in it. In memory of Alexei, the last Tsar of Russia, who in death became the hero of all or at least most. But in front of it there is one big change. The massive statue to Alexei, sitting above Alexei's grave. Seeing it had a very profound impact on Alexei, as he seemed to be a bit in a state of shock when he first came up to it. But then he recovered himself.

Alexei, "You know, I'm not sure if that statue quite captures me, but the really weird thing is I'm both up here and down there at the same time, De De De De De De De," as he smirked at me. Clearly in Santa Cruz, Alexei had watched one too many Twilight Zones.

Then we walked in the door, and hanging in the glass case from the ceiling, was Alexei's army uniform, completely stained in the blood that had soaked it. Alexei, like at his grave, seemed taken back a bit before he braced himself.

Me, "You know people have offered millions for that uniform."

Alexei, "Remind me to bleed on something for you, it should more than cover our trip."

As we walked around, Alexei noted how amazing it was, so many years have passed, but it looks like it did when he left it, but that of course he didn't realize when he left it that last time, he would never see it again. His eyes looked a little watery. We saw the palace chapel room where Alexei had prayed, the Great Semi-Circular Hall where Alexei had watched his movies, and the Mountain Room with the wooden slide. Next to the wooden slide, was Alexei's charming miniature gas powered car his parents had given him, he had so loved as a child.

Alexei, with a mischievous look on his face, "I would take you for a ride, but we might get in trouble."

People kept on looking at Alexei curiously. At the Alexander Palace people clearly had Alexei on their mind, and Alexei looked very much like Alexei. Now I know what he meant by coming to haunt the Alexander Palace. One of the museum attendants even came up and by looking at us, or overhearing us, clearly thought we spoke English.

Attendant, "You are the spitting image of Tsar Alexei."

Alexei chuckling, "I get that a lot."

Attendant, "Are you of relation?"

Alexei, "Distant cousin, my name is Alexei Derevenko."

Attendant looking at Alexei puzzled, "Amazing, you are even named after him, and you know Derevenko was the name of his doctor, Vladimir. Vladimir's son Kolya was Alexei's best friend."

Alexei, "Hmm, now that is interesting, quite the coincidence now I think of it."

After Alexei warmly said farewell to his new friend, we headed up to Alexei's rooms.

We went to Alexei's classroom, the place where he was initially abducted by the Provisional Government so many years ago, it felt chilling.

Alexei, "Mr. Gilliard, and the tutor assigned me by the Provisional Government, Boris Tolstoy, I have to give both credit, taught me well. One thing I have to give the Liberals, is they did teach me to think for myself. They just didn't realize that thinking for myself didn't exactly mean agreeing with them on everything. Without Boris, I'm not sure I would have ever stood up to Mr. Kerensky. I kind of doubt that is what Mr. Kerensky had planned."

Me, "What inspired you to stand up to Kerensky?"

Alexei, "I knew I had to see my family and help my people. I knew I had to have the courage to do what I felt was right. But I also knew Mr. Kerensky wasn't going to hurt me. He had done everything he could to keep me comfortable, he had brought his two sons along with the sons of other liberal Duma members over to keep me company. He treated me a bit like a son. But he also needed me. You don't kill the golden goose. I realized this was my power."

Alexei certainly was not dumb.

We walked into Alexei's bedroom. I could tell Alexei was really beginning to feel at home. The chess set that Alexei used sat on the table, only recently returned in Sergei's will. Apparently, Sergei had taken the original and kept it as something to remember Alexei by.

Alexei grinning, "I would invite you over, we could play a game of chess, but I get the sense the museum attendants wouldn't like it, this place though mine, is not really mine anymore, it now belongs to the people. When I told Kerensky I wanted to dispose of surplus royal property, the Alexander Palace was not on the list, but then I guess this is the only way the place would exist here like this today."

Looking at the chess set I asked Alexei, "That last chess game you played with Sergei, Sergei always wondered if he really beat you, or if you let him win."

Alexei, "That is a mystery you shall never know."

I saw all the saints and religious paraphernalia on the wooden ikon stand and was getting a sense of how Alexei had ended up so religious.

Then we walked into Alexei's playroom, you could tell Alexei had many fond memories of it, and I was astounded with how many toys he had.

Alexei, "There are advantages to being the Tsesarevich."

We then walked out onto the grounds, that had been Alexei's playground in life, and you could feel something spiritual come over him.

Alexei, "You know this is where I spent much of my time, when not in my studies, after I was returned to the Alexander Palace and my family was shipped to Livadia, I really only used my suite of rooms and a few of the common rooms. I left my parents' and sisters' rooms somewhat untouched in honor of my family, but I couldn't resist Papa's swimming bathtub. It was here on the grounds I truly was in paradise."

Alexei then went on to tell me all the tales of his time out here as we walked out to the Children's Island and sat in the playhouse.

Alexei, "We used to strip our clothes and swim over here, but with all the people around I doubt we would be allowed to do it," as Alexei smiled his mischievous grin.

Me, "You know, you were saying you would like to have me over, that is possible, we got the time charm. We go back to the train, you say I'm some American guy you met, I mean you are the Tsar, you don't get out in Ekaterinburg, you don't get shot, and we go back to the Alexander Palace where you will be safe."

Alexei, "I would love to have you, but I don't think that will work. You know what happened last time you tried to alter history. You practically altered yourself out of existence."

Me, "But last time I shot at you to get the guards to

rush you to safety before the real killers could get you. And Kerensky takes you back. This time there will be no shooting, you will go back freely."

Alexei, "You want me to go hide in the Alexander Palace while my people are suffering? Our soldiers who fought so bravely in World War I didn't go and hide, but you want me their leader to go do so?"

Me, "Yeah, but then you would be alive, you are the Tsar, your survival is more important to the country than some soldier."

Alexei, "But you pretty much told me each further year I live, really doesn't change a lot, the Bolsheviks still win, I'm still ultimately murdered. But because the Communists go into the next World War weaker, the war goes on longer, and millions more people die, including your own grandfather."

Me, "You die because you will not stop standing up to them, maybe if you just stopped, you could live."

Alexei, "But that doesn't change the fact that my existence ends up creating more suffering in the next World War. You really believe my life is worth more than our soldiers who died in World War I, you really believe my life is worth more than the millions more who will go on to die in my place in the next World War, so I can maybe live?"

I was speechless by this point, Alexei was so often of little words, he rarely argued, but wow, he had me in checkmate, I then just out of exasperation shouted, "Yes!" Alexei then had nothing else to say as he stared off into the distance.

After a few minutes Alexei chimed in. "You wanted to come to Russia James, let's enjoy it, this is a discussion we can continue later." And we just sat there on the island in silence, like he used to do with Sergei and Kolya. Well with the tourists milling around, not quite silence. I felt a sense of unease as I realized for the first time that Alexei really was contemplating going back to be shot, I mean who the fuck, would do that, but I was glad Alexei said we could continue this discussion. Maybe I had a chance of talking him out of it.

After that we went out to the White Tower to see the view of the surrounding grounds and community, a view Alexei said always brought him great inspiration, as we looked out in awe.

Then we went down to the Pushkin train station to tour the train that took Alexei on his fateful journey that has now become such a famous part of Russian and world history. The journey of the kind, charismatic boy Tsar who had he lived just might have saved Russia and the world.

Alexei, "It looks just like it did the last I saw it a few weeks ago, this is amazing. My newspapers are even still on the table, though they have aged a bit."

I was in awe with the history, and then we looked at

Alexei's sleeping compartment from where I had taken him a few weeks earlier. It did look exactly how it looked when I last saw it.

Alexei, "Well here is where we met, you know I thought you were a nut, but you seemed rather harmless, so I figured it might be a bit amusing to humor you."

Me, "Little did you know. When the old guy in the suit gave me the time charm in the first place and suggested I go back and save you, I thought he was a nut."

Alexei, "By the way, do you know whatever happened to my dog Joy?"

Me, "When your family came up to your funeral, they took Joy with them to Livadia and then into exile in England."

Alexei softly smiled, "I am glad."

As we got out, we noticed a train tour was going to do Alexei's exact route, though not on the old royal train now a museum and landmark of course, but on a more modern train, with even an Alexei actor to lead the tour. It would arrive in Ekaterinburg on July 17th, 77 years after that tragic day. I suggested we take it.

Alexei in his mocking tone, "You have spent all this time trying to keep me away from Ekaterinburg and now you want to go to Ekaterinburg?"

Me, "We could get off before Ekaterinburg, we don't

have to go to Ekaterinburg."

Alexei grinning, "This is your trip James, I'm at your command."

We booked the English version then hung out in Pushkin a little bit. Alexei lamented that we couldn't go up and stay the night at his place. We then went over and saw the truly outlandish Catherine Palace, by far much grander than the Alexander Palace preferred by Alexei and his family. The Catherine Palace almost made the Alexander Palace seem middle class. Alexei remarked that the Catherine Palace really was too much and was exactly what he had in mind when he proposed liquidating excess royal property to help the people.

Alexei went by Kolya's apartment in the service wing. The outside looked much as it did in the early 20th, century, but the inside had been gutted for other uses. Mr. Gilliard would often drive Alexei to visit Kolya after his studies. The only friend Alexei got to regularly visit his home. Alexei said they had great fun, and it was refreshing to be out of the palace.

We were staying at a little place in Pushkin that night when Alexei had the most brilliant idea ever.

Alexei, "You know when I was lamenting, we couldn't stay at my place tonight, well we got the time travel charm, I knew it would come in handy, let's do it."

Me, "Really!"

Alexei, "Yeah, if we get there after my court and I have left on the train journey, no one will likely be there. The guards usually patrolled the perimeter, and Kerensky had me on very limited staff. I had never gotten the opportunity to increase it after I stood up to him. But we will need to be careful we're not seen, people will think I am supposed to be on the train, and you're an intruder. And you must promise me, we will come back when I say we do."

Me, "I promise."

Alexei put on his uniform, and I put on my dress clothes, still a little off, but not as off as the polo shirt, jeans, and sneakers. And with that we got out the charm, and we were off to the night of June 30th, during the glorious summer of 1923, in Alexei's bedroom. And there we were. Alexei put on one of his night gowns and gave me a spare then we slept in Alexei's bed together, like he had with Sergei. It was magical.

The next morning, we got up, Alexei gave me a spare shirt and pants of his that looked a little more contemporary. Alexei was taller than me, so it was a little big, but it worked. I had to keep my shoes as Alexei's feet were smaller and his shoes wouldn't fit.

Alexei, assembled breakfast, boiled eggs, bread, butter, and milk, it was quite simple for the Tsar of Russia, my breakfasts were fancier than his. He said he would have made me blini, but he didn't really know how to cook. Alexei's chess set was on the train, so Alexei got the chess set out of his father's room and we took it back to his bedroom to play. He beat me once again. If he let Sergei win, I guess he wasn't going to give me the same luxury. Then we walked into Alexei's playroom and checked out all of his cool toys. They were simpler than the toys today but were still a lot of fun. We went out on the grounds and Alexei introduced me to his cat Kotka and his donkey Vanka. Alexei was curious if I knew their fate. I told him I thought Vanka passed away not long after he did, but that Kotka I believe was taken by Alexei's family. Alexei was glad they had good lives. I didn't get to meet Joy since Joy was on the train with the 1923 Alexei.

We fooled around on the grounds being careful not to be seen, it almost felt like we were in the woods. And then we stripped our clothes and swam out to the Children's Island, lounging around the playhouse with the leather upholstered furniture, and then out on the grass in the sun. Alexei was more relaxed than I had ever seen him. We did not talk, we just hung out there in silence, like him and Sergei often did, it felt touched by God. As I was here at the Alexander Palace with the flesh and blood Alexei, it was more magical than even in my dreams. I could have done this forever.

We did the same routine for several days, eating what we could scrounge up, Alexei not knowing how to cook, and I not being familiar with a Russian kitchen from 1923. Alexei thought about making a bonfire but figured that would draw too much attention. Then we always prayed before bed. After our last day, we spent our final moments at the Children's Island, and then Alexei made clear it was time we returned. I didn't want to, but Alexei reminded me I promised, and that we had tinkered with history long enough. And with that we went up to Alexei's bedroom, I had tears in my eyes, but Alexei kindly put his arm around me in silence, he was so comforting, and then we were back in our hotel room in Pushkin.

Chapter 10

We went down to the train station for the tour. Alexei had a good chat with the tour conductor who was playing Alexei. The tour conductor thought Alexei looked more like Alexei than he did and should consider going into the field of Alexei actors. Alexei remarked to me privately that he didn't think the conductor totally looked like him. As we sat down Alexei remembered how Oleg joined him on his journey, that he had always liked Oleg but didn't know if Oleg was just spying for his father, but that Oleg turned out to be a great friend, and a crucial advisor, and in the end, Oleg was the most useful to him of all.

And then the train was off, like in Alexei's original journey it went straight to Livadia where Alexei saw his family for the last time before it tracked back on Alexei's fateful journey through Ukraine, Belorussia, then turning towards Moscow before eventually ending up on that tragic day in Ekaterinburg. Ukraine and Belorussia were now independent countries and Alexei spent much of the time lamenting about the break-up of the old Russian Empire. Alexei truly believed that the many different groups could have lived together in peace much like the diverse groups in the United States live together in peace.

Livadia had been used for varying purposes over the

years since Alexei's family fled Russia. While it had been restored, it looked different than the way Alexei remembered it. I could tell he felt kind of sad. As he told me Livadia was paradise for Russia, it's how he imagined heaven. We got a little bit of free time and went out to the beach Alexei so loved. And we were even able to slip off a bit and do a little skinny dipping, just the way Alexei remembered it.

We went to Yalta where Alexei had given his first speech after the famous one at the Alexander Palace, and we were off to the varying destinations Alexei had visited on his famous tour through Russia. There was a plaque at each place Alexei visited and our tour guide reenacted Alexei's speeches. The speeches were practically the same with little touches added in for various communities.

Me, "You need to mix up your speech a bit more."

Alexei with his famous smile, "Why would I want to mix up perfection."

Alexei's remarks to the Jewish community at the Synagogue in Minsk was a little more different, geared towards tolerance and all citizens of the Russian Empire being equal under the eyes of the law. The current Rabbi at the synagogue let the group know how much that moment had meant to them, a Russian Tsar engaging them. It was magical to a group of people who had spent years of oppression under the Russian Empire. Alexei was clearly touched by the effect he had.

When we rolled into Moscow, we saw Red Square and St. Basil's Cathedral where Alexei had his biggest turnout. Alexei said they were all in high spirits that day, it was such a triumph. But quite often Alexei seemed a bit distant, lost in his thoughts. The poor peasant village that Alexei had been brought out to was now a museum. You felt their simple impoverished lives from a bygone era. Alexei's speech to them again had been a little more different hitting on the need for land reform, and a welfare system to alleviate the suffering of the Russian poor. It was also here that inspired Alexei's plan to sell excess royal property.

Alexei, "You know these people were truly a shock for all of us. Oleg, Kolya, even Sergei. We were all sheltered Petrograd boys. Never before had we truly seen such poverty close up. With all my heart I wanted to help these people." Alexei's eyes looked a bit moist.

Then we rolled into the station where the first assassination attempt against Alexei had occurred. And the tour guide went over the famous story about Alexei, in all his love and kindness, forgiving his would-be assassin. Alexei seemed a little bored.

Then Jack a guy who looked similar to our age, the descendent of Russian emigres, who was taking the tour with his mother spoke up, with a bit of a cavalier voice and a

smart-alecky smile, "The goody two shoes sounds too dumb
to live, no wonder somebody got his ass."

People looked at him like what the fuck was wrong
with him. His mother asked him to be respectful. I wanted to
knock that smirk right off his face. How could someone seem
happy that someone killed Alexei. Alexei seemed unfazed.

Tour Conductor respectfully, "The legacy of Alexei is
debated, some argue that he was hopelessly naïve and
needlessly and continuously exposed himself to danger. There
are those who argue that the surprise is not that he was killed,
but that he managed to survive as long as he did against the
violent backdrop of the Russian Revolution. But it must also
be remembered that Alexei had lived a very sheltered life, first
as the sickly Tsesarevich then as the figurehead Tsar under
the custody of the Provisional government. He might not
have fully appreciated the mood the country was in."

Alexei quipped in, "The attempt that guy made to kill
Alexei was weak, to try and shoot Alexei in front of an armed
guard. Maybe Alexei thought it seemed more an act of
desperation than a serious attempt. No one was harmed,
maybe Alexei figured you cannot have a crime without a
victim."

Tour Conductor smiling at Alexei, "You know that is
pretty close to the argument Alexei made."

Once back on the train, Alexei sat down next to Jack

and regaled him with tales of Alexei's childhood pranks and other antics. Jack was enthralled and laughed much of the time. Alexei was clearly making a new friend. Jack may not have been a fan of Saint Alexei, but he clearly liked Alexei.

When Alexei came back and sat down with me, his spirits seemed oddly lifted.

Me, "You actually like that guy, he was a jerk."

Alexei, "He's a good guy, I think he actually kind of lightened the mood a little bit."

I offered we get off the tour before Ekaterinburg, I had already had quite enough of Ekaterinburg, but Alexei said this tour was my idea, but we started it, and now he was going to finish it. Alexei then turned to me somberly, "I do not know why they had to kill me. I would have worked with anyone."

Me, "You were good, they were evil."

Alexei looked at me warmly.

Then we got off in Ekaterinburg on July 17th and the tour guide gave Alexei's final speech. Then went over Alexei's legacy of love, warmth, kindness, empathy, hope and how much he meant to the Russian people and the world, and how much better of a place this world would be if we only followed Alexei.

Jack, "When are we going to get to see the reenactment of the do gooder getting shot, and bleeding all over his friends? That would be entertaining."

The rest of us looked at Jack with disgust, in that moment I wanted to shoot him. Alexei seemed unfazed.

Tour Conductor, "We do not do a reenactment of the shooting as part of this tour."

Jack, "Did Alexei piss and crap his pants when he died. Did his friends smell a giant turd?"

Jack's mom was pleading with him to knock it off, I was about to get up, but Alexei held my hand, and I knew he didn't want me to confront him. Alexei whispered in my ear that reminded him to make sure he used the toilet that morning.

Alexei then said sympathetically to the group, as if trying to lower the temperature, "Alexei was only human, bodily functions are a human response."

Jack looked at Alexei, not sure what to make of Alexei's remark.

Then the tour guide spoke up, "That has not been recorded by history."

The tour guide then invited the group to give their opinions on Alexei's legacy, and it was diverse, some saw him as a Monarchist, some as a Liberal, some even as leaning towards the Communists. The most popular theory on his murder has always been that Lenin did it, and co-opted his legacy, it is what I believed, and Alexei saw as the most plausible scenario, but some thought the Monarchists had killed him fearing that Alexei was leaning too far to the left. And even one person suggested Kerensky had him killed as Alexei slipped from his control. The Kerensky suggestion earned an eye roll from Alexei, who obviously didn't believe that Kerensky would have hurt him.

When everyone was done, Alexei then chimed in, "Maybe Alexei was a human being who liked people, and cared for them, and wanted to see them happy and at peace. Maybe Alexei was tired of the ideologues and politicians who were tearing apart his country and took his message directly to the people. Maybe Alexei felt that he could not hide away in cowardice when so many Russian soldiers had given their lives in The Great War. Maybe Alexei tried to have the courage to do what was right and put his faith in God, that his will would be done."

The crowd was moved by Alexei's thoughts on Alexei.

Tour Conductor, "You really once again captured, what Alexei would have likely said. You would be great at my job."

Alexei just laughed.

Then the tour conductor let us know we would be visiting the final destination on the tour. The Church of St. Alexei. Which earned a strong eye roll from Alexei. The

Church of St. Alexei near the site of Alexei's assassination was amazing with the statues of Alexei and paintings of Alexei. A holy relic held by the church was a handkerchief that a local peasant had dipped in the pool of blood left on the platform after Alexei was shot.

Our tour guide said that some miracles had been credited to Alexei, and that people would pray before his statue asking for him to intercede on their behalf with God. That while not official Church doctrine, some even suggested that Alexei was the innocent sacrifice sent by God to atone for Russia's sins. Through much of this Alexei seemed in great thought. Jack was respectful and behaved himself. And the tour was over. Alexei thanked the tour guide for putting on such a great show but let him know we would not be going back with the group to St. Petersburg.

He then asked Jack if he wanted to hang out for a few hours with us before the group went back. I wasn't looking forward to hanging out with Jack, but what could I say. Jack's mother seemed a little concerned that they didn't really know us, but Jack made clear he was 18 and could do as he pleased. Alexei promised Jack's mom we would take good care of him, to Jack's displeasure.

Chapter 11

We went out and ended up having Port Wine and Blini. And Jack and Alexei had great fun bantering back and forth. Then Alexei just could not resist.

Alexei, "What would you say if I told you I was Tsar Alexei Nikolaevich Romanov?"

Jack looking amused, "You're too cool to be Alexei, anyhow I would say you're insane."

Alexei, "The insanity part is a fair assessment. James, do you think we should show Jack our little secret?"

Jack was starting to look a little perplexed, and I was starting to feel a little sick to the stomach.

Me, "If you're thinking what I think you're thinking, it is a very, very bad idea. You have never taken it this far before."

Alexei, "I have never met someone yet, whom I felt could benefit from it like Jack here."

At which point I slipped, "Jack has fantasies of you dead, laying in your own piss and shit, I think he is the last person we need to share this with."

Alexei looked a little concerned with what I said, and a little hurt that he didn't feel I was playing along.

Jack, "You guys really are nuts."

Alexei, "Come with us, we need a private place for

this."

Jack, "I'm really not gay."

Alexei, "That's good, I'm not either. But if that interests you, you can always ask James if he would like to play along."

Me, "I think that port has gone to your brain."

Alexei, "James please trust me. Jack, I really can't ask you to trust us, since you don't know us, but I promise an experience you will never forget, we're not going to hurt you, we are unarmed, you're a good-sized guy, worst case scenario you will get a good laugh at how crazy we are. Let's go get a hotel room so we can put the luggage somewhere."

Jack, "My mom is going to worry if I'm gone too long."

Alexei, "I promise we will have you back before you know we are gone."

With that we got a room. And Alexei got out the time charm. I knew what he had in mind, and we started stripping to change our clothes.

Jack "I knew you guys were gay."

Alexei smiling, "You guys in the future are sure obsessed with the concept of being gay."

Alexei then put his full uniform on.

Jack, "Oh my God, you really do think you're the last Russian Tsar."

Alexei just smiled, I didn't like any of this, but I could never say no to Alexei. I then grasped the time charm with Alexei.

Alexei, "Jack you have to touch us, and not in the way you're likely thinking. Come hold my hand."

Jack, "You're nuts," he then grasped Alexei's hand.

Alexei, "James take us to the afternoon of July 7th, 1923, my bedroom at the Alexander Palace."

And with that I did.

Jack was clearly in a state of utter shock at first, I thought we might have to rush him back to the future for an emergency room. I mean what if we killed him when he was last seen with me, I could never go back. Alexei grabbed him and laid him down on his bed, though didn't seem too concerned.

Me, "I just wanted to beat him up, not kill him, this is a little extreme for insulting you."

Alexei chuckled smiling at me, "Have you not learned anything James, trust in God."

As Jack came to, he clearly wondered if this was a dream, was he crazy, had we slipped him drugs. Then he begged us not to rape him.

Alexei then sat down on his bed, holding Jack's hand with incredible kindness, empathy, and warmth that Alexei just radiated and explained exactly everything as he knew it, me coming to collect him, how he felt many of the same emotions, how impossible this seems, but it is proof in something beyond the physical world. I never really thought about it like that. I just shrugged my head, not knowing what to make of all this. What was Alexei doing, Alexei was always the one saying we could not just mess around with time as we pleased.

Alexei then made clear to him he would like to show Jack around the 1923 Alexander Palace, but that he was supposed to be on the train with his court, and that no one was supposed to be here, so we needed to keep a low profile. That the guards patrolled the perimeter, so if we were careful, it should be cool. But that we could not be seen, and that if he misbehaved that I would have to tackle him and take him back to the future.

Jack, "Okay, I'm really not sure what to think, but as I said, my mom will start worrying about me."

Alexei, "Time does not travel at the same pace in the loop, we can spend as long as we want, take you back to the moment we took you, and no one will know you were gone."

Jack, "Okay, I might as well play along, looking at all the saints and religious paraphernalia on the ikon stand, you really are quite religious."

Alexei, "Yes, I'm a believer in Christ."

Jack, "My grandparents were very Russian Orthodox.

I always thought it was a bunch of superstition."

Alexei, "If you can believe in time travel you can believe in God. In fact, I first thought I was in paradise, not the future."

Jack, "I'm not sure if I believe in this."

Alexei, "Fair enough."

Alexei then gave Jack the grand tour, as he clearly recognized it as the Alexander Palace, from the Museum he had just seen, but now it was clearly Alexei's home without the modern trappings. With the sheer authenticity of it all you could tell he was beginning to wonder if we were telling him the truth. We went into Alexei's playroom where Alexei showed him his toys.

Jack, "You were quite the rich kid."

Alexei, "Clear advantages to being the Tsesarevich."

We then went out on the grounds that Alexei so loved and introduced Jack to Kotka and Vanka. He apologized that Jack couldn't meet Joy, but Joy was on the train with the 1923 Alexei.

Jack, "How can you be here and on the train?"

Alexei, "I really don't know, but I was clearly in the year 2000 while my body lay in the grave, so it just is."

Then we went out towards the island.

Alexei, "Let's strip our clothes and swim out."

Jack, "I knew you boys wanted to play some strange

sex games.”

Alexei rolling his eyes, “Why is all you people in the future can talk about is sex. Not sure if you guys are really as advanced as you think you are.”

Jack, “Anyhow, I would prefer to keep my clothes on.”

Alexei, “It’s okay,” he then led Jack over to the bridge, something we never used, and we walked over to the playhouse on the children’s island and sat on the leather upholstered furniture.

Jack turned to me, “You really are very quiet.”

Me, “That is because I don’t really like you.”

Alexei chuckling, “Now that is rude James, knock it off.”

Jack then turned to Alexei, “You really are quite bossy.”

Alexei, “I’m the Tsar, I guess I come by it naturally.”

Jack, “Alexei, can I ask you a question.”

Alexei, “Sure.”

Jack, “Why were you such a goody two shoes? I mean you really seem like a fun guy, though I’m not so sure about James.”

Alexei, “James is a great guy, you just have to get to know him. And what is wrong with trying to be good? Would you prefer I was a baddy two shoes? And what is it with the two shoes? Who has only one shoe? I'm just a human being, I like to have fun, and I can only take being serious for so long. But if you want me to be a bad guy, James and I could just drown you out in the pond if you would prefer."

Jack, "Why did you forgive the guy who tried to kill you. That is just weird."

Alexei was quiet for a moment, "As I already made clear, he didn't hurt me, how can we punish someone for a crime they didn't commit. Maybe he never really intended to kill me. We will never know since he didn't actually get the opportunity to pull the trigger. My countrymen have suffered so much. Maybe if you were in his shoes, you would've tried to kill me too."

Jack, "You really are not of this world, but I'm sorry I disrespected you. I'm sorry they hurt you. My family has always so revered you. If I misbehaved my grandma would ask me, "What would Alexei do?" I just thought it was weird when they didn't even know you, and you kind of seemed too good to be true."

Alexei "Yeah on that tour I thought I sounded too good to be true too, anyhow thank you for reminding me of the importance of using the restroom before getting shot."

Jack, "I didn't really mean that."

Then Alexei got up, hands out for a bear hug.

Jack, "I would prefer not."

Alexei, "Come on, for me, you can make it up to me for insulting me, I'm fully clothed, so you can put away your dirty thoughts."

He then got up and gently hugged Alexei, as Alexei bear hugged him.

Alexei, "Come over here James, group hug."

And with that I embraced Alexei, and this odd, strange guy that for some reason Alexei decided to bring home like some lost puppy.

Jack, "You know if the people who shot you, got to know you, I don't see how they could hurt you."

Alexei, "I met Vladimir Lenin once, he pretty much indirectly threatened to kill me, and it looks like he most likely did just that. Apparently, some are immune to my charm."

Jack, "But now you know your fate you can change it."

Alexei, "Don't worry about me, I still have some time left." Alexei then sat back down, "Let's have some silence boys, this place is best enjoyed in silence."

Jack, "You really are used to getting your way."

Alexei, "Yes I am."

After a while since we had three people, we played Nain Jaune, one of Alexei's favorite games, a French card game played on a board. It is also called Yellow Dwarf.

When we were done Alexei turned to Jack, "We

better get you home, we have taken enough of your time, but thank you for entertaining us."

Jack, "No, thank you, this experience has been out of this world, I still don't know what to think of it."

Alexei, "It may take some time to process."

With that we headed back to Alexei's bedroom, then the hotel room. Alexei gave Jack another hug. Alexei sometimes could just not stop hugging people, then said to Jack, "I trust you will keep our secret unless you desire to spend some time in a mental institution, my friend."

Jack, "I will my friend."

Chapter 12

And with that Jack was off, and Alexei had added a new friend to his lengthy collection. Then he turned to me. "I want to spend my remaining time with you, let's go home, well to my home."

I was ecstatic, maybe Alexei had finally seen the light, and we were just going to hang out together forever. And with that we went back to the 1923 Alexander Palace.

When we went to sleep that night, Alexei did something he had never done before. He turned around and put his arms around my chest gripping me firmly, as if I was his teddy bear. I could feel his warm breath on the back of my neck. I felt so at peace, I loved him so much. During the day we played games, hung out with Alexei's pets, minus of course Joy, who I was sad I wasn't going to get to meet. We frolicked on the interior of the grounds, careful to avoid being spotted by the guards, and swam out to Alexei's island. I had studied how to make blini on the computer before we left, and Alexei and I figured out the 1923 kitchen. It was a detached building near the street, but we used the underground passage to avoid detection. We ate a lot of blini and drank a lot of port and champagne. It was the most magical time of my life. And each night Alexei held me tight.

Then came Saturday, Alexei made clear after sundown

that he would no longer be able to eat until communion the next morning, observing the Orthodox fast, so we should especially enjoy that day. Alexei said that while I couldn't take communion until I officially became a member of the church, he would very much like me to otherwise join him in the process. As night fell, we zipped back to the future and Alexei was confessed in full uniform by a priest at the Church of St. Alexei. Alexei asked the Priest what he thought about all of this, was Alexei truly the atonement for Russia's sins. The Priest was subtle, telling Alexei that Alexei was clearly a force for good, and was a man of great faith, and that his martyrdom had earned him sainthood, but he couldn't really go beyond that. That some believe Alexei may have been more, but that is a mystery only known by God. And then we zipped back to the 1923 Alexander Palace where we prayed for several hours before bed.

The next morning we went back to the future, to the church of St. Alexei with Alexei in full uniform. People clearly took note, but likely thought Alexei was one of many actors playing Alexei. The focus of the Liturgy was not Alexei, but Jesus Christ. Alexei received Communion, then we went back to the 1923 Alexander Palace. We went out to the playhouse, not skinny dipping like we normally did, but Alexei walking the bridge, something he never did. Then sitting down in the place we so loved, his eyes clearly watering, turned to me.

Alexei, "James, my dear friend, we need to talk."

I felt the world crashing down around me. I felt the impending doom. He didn't need to say a word. I remembered his story of St. Peter, and of all the brave Russian soldiers who had given their lives for their country. And his question to me, if millions should die so he could live. My answer was the same, yes, yes, yes, yes, yes. He was so special, I loved him so much. I knew our time was coming to an end. And I just started wailing as I broke down in tears.

Alexei sat down next to me and put his arm around me, "Please my friend, if you ever loved me, don't make this harder."

And then with every ounce of willpower and courage in my body, my gut truly aching in pain, I stopped crying, and with my red eyes looked towards Alexei's handsome face, with those piercing blue eyes so contrasting to his auburn brown hair.

Alexei, "We must have the courage to do what is right, I am not going to run away from the cross, I am not going to cower when so many of our brave soldiers died valiantly in my name. I am not going to let millions die so I can live, and if you love me, you will respect my decision."

Me, "What if I told you I lied, that you must live so millions will not die?"

Alexei, "I would believe you are now lying to me whom you claim is your best friend and you love."

Me, "Then I will not do so."

Alexei, "Thank you."

Me, "When did you decide?"

Alexei, "After the first night, when it was clear I couldn't have my friends and family, and the sheer pain I felt at the devastation my murder caused to those I so loved. I knew I was not in heaven, that you must have been telling me the truth, somehow you had brought me into the future. That next morning when I woke up, I knew what I was going to do. But your world seemed so entertaining, I was so curious, and you seemed so alone, like you really needed a friend. I figured destiny could wait. I owed myself a little fun."

Me, "You do not have to get out on that platform, you could save us those of us who love you that pain you were talking about."

Alexei, "James, I beg you, do not do this to me."

Me, "I am sorry."

Alexei, "Through a touch of magic, I have seen the promised land, and gotten to touch it, if even for a brief time. I have also seen my legacy. I failed to save my country, but you came all the way from Santa Cruz California in the year 2000 to save my life. I told Mr. Kerensky that Russia needed hope, and in that simple goal for my country and the world I exceeded my wildest dreams. Maybe this is the best I can do. Maybe I must trust in God."

I was speechless.

Alexei went on, "I love you James, I want you to go to Church, it will come to you in time, in that I have faith. I want you to try and do good. I want you to try and be good. I want you to try and have the courage to do what is right. I look forward to seeing you again someday in heaven. I will introduce you to my monkey."

I felt so drained, I didn't know what to say. I loved him so much, but he had shut me down, as if somehow my protests would violate our friendship. I didn't know what to do.

Alexei pulled a huge diamond ring out of his pocket. "Take this James, it should cover our trip."

I looked at it in shock, "I can't take that from you, I don't want it, the trip is on me, you gave me so much more than a diamond ring could ever cover."

Alexei, "I want you to have it, I was going to have Kerensky sell excess royal property anyway, but he made clear it will hardly be a drop in the bucket for the suffering of the people. And if you don't take it, the Commies will likely get it. I want you to have it," as he shoved it in my pocket.

Me, "Did you always know you were going to give this to me? Why didn't you tell me?"

Alexei, "I wanted you to take me out of the kindness of your heart, and you did. I was musing to my friends shortly before you came to get me about how I would like to see the Pacific Ocean, meet our Muslim subjects, and ultimately visit New York, the Holy Land and Japan. We did all of those, well maybe I didn't meet Muslim Russians, but I did meet Muslims. You were like a guardian angel come to grant me my wishes before I met my fate."

I was astounded.

Alexei pulled out the time charm. "Now I want you to take me back, not to midnight but to 7:30 that morning, that is about the time I would have gotten up. I don't wish to sleep there. Then once you are safely home, I want you to destroy that charm. We can't have you going back to save Jesus now. I am grateful for what is done, but time is not meant to be tinkered with."

I just sat there.

Alexei, "Please my friend, I'm ready."

I then stuck it in my pocket, hugged him, and took us back to his sleeping car.

Alexei, hugged me, "I love you my friend, but now you must go, see you again in paradise. I trust you will be gone before anyone finds you, now it is time for my final act." With that Alexei's famous smile came across his face, and it seemed as if none of this had happened.

Me, "I love you, you changed my life forever, you mean more to me than you will ever know."

Alexei smiled back at me as he was preparing to exit the door. "Now I must really go use the toilet." And with that he was gone.

I didn't go back, but I went more parallel, as I put myself below the platform outside of the train, where the crowds would watch Alexei give his final speech. It was about two hours, and it felt like each moment was an eternity. I saw a figure that looked like Oleg wander over to the train station, to what I knew was to call his father and get the news of Lenin's offer to negotiate with Alexei. The news that I knew had so excited them that morning.

Then the crowds grew, and Alexei came out as charismatic and radiant as ever, giving, like in history, the best speech he ever gave. He seemed to truly relish the moment. It was just like it had always been. Then he came down from the platform and waded into the crowds, shaking hands, hugging, listening to their concerns, he seemed to be enjoying this as if he only had moments to live. And I remembered how he had spent even longer than usual in the crowd in Ekaterinburg. Had he always known, were we forever going through some loop in time? He had so shut down any debate about the sincerity of Lenin's overture that morning, accepting it at what seemed face value.

He then deviated from history, as he shook my hand
with that radiant smile. He then hugged me, whispering in my
ear, "Promise me you will destroy it, James."

Me, "I promise, I love you."

Alexei, "I love you too James."

And with that he walked off lifting that now famous
kid and shouting the future of Russia, a future he knew he
wouldn't see. You could tell he didn't want to leave the
crowds, as he was savoring every last minute of his life on
earth.

He then ascended to the platform where he was
joined by Sergei, Kolya, and Oleg, as they basked in their
victory, Lenin was going to negotiate, Alexei had won, Alexei
had saved Russia, but I knew Alexei clearly knew otherwise.

Then that first shot rang out, piercing my heart.
Alexei grasped his stomach, as his friends looked at him with
puzzled looks. Then that second shot rang out, shattering my
heart, as Alexei grabbed his chest and collapsed. Sergei
cradled Alexei as Kolya sat down next to him. Kolya looked
like he wanted to grab Alexei's body from Sergei. Oleg
kneeled holding his hand. I remembered Alexei's last words
to his friends that he would see them in heaven and to trust
in God. Had he thought these out? Then Sergei started
wailing the shrillest wail I had ever heard. Kolya was crying in
his arms, and Oleg was calling Alexei's name over and over

again, as if he would awaken, while he bled out. I knew he was gone. I felt like my heart was gone, and I vomited right there. How could there be such evil in this world, this force of love, slain by evil. I wanted to go up and be with them, but I knew I couldn't. Joy came running out towards his master.

I then walked around behind the train station and went back to our hotel in Ekaterinburg. I cried, and I cried, and I cried some more until I passed out asleep. I held the clothes he had worn to my face to pick up his scent. Only in my dreams could I see my dear friend again. Then I woke up and started crying. I couldn't eat. I just cried. I was so exhausted. I felt like I wanted to die, and then maybe I would be up in heaven with Alexei and his monkey forever.

I went to the gas station next door to get a canister of gas to fulfill Alexei's final wish. How I wanted to go back and collect Alexei again, but I knew I couldn't. If I showed up after our encounter, I knew he would not go. If I showed up before our encounter, my dear friend would have to get to know me all over again. Maybe we could just loop forever, but I knew it couldn't be, if I loved him, I had to respect his wishes. I then set the time charm on fire out behind the hotel, cutting off any possibility of ever seeing him in this world again. But it didn't burn, it just disappeared into thin air, it truly was magic, but was clearly no longer mine. My Alexei was gone forever. What was he, who was he, this bright shining comet that blazed through the Russian sky, and through my life, if only for the briefest time.

I then went to the Church of St. Alexei and dropped before his statue. The cold statue didn't truly capture him, his love, his warmth, his fun-loving personality. "I love you Alexei, I love you, can you hear me Alexei, I love you, I love you, I love you." Sometimes you have to believe in miracles, sometimes you have to believe in God.

Author's Epilogue

Now we have seen the tale of Alexei according to James. The fantasies of a lonely young man dreaming of his idol, or maybe there is a bit of magic in this universe beyond the understanding of science.

Alexei in our stories clearly touched those around him, very much like the real Alexei of history. Those with great talents can use those talents for good or evil. Alexei chose good.